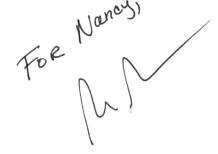

For Nancy,

BROKEN
OPEN

BROKEN
OPEN

an erotic novella

by

Robin Reinach

Central Park Publishers

Published in the United States

Central Park Publishers
New York, NY
www.centralparkpublishers.com

*This book is a work of fiction. Names, characters, places and incidents
are either the product of the author's imagination or are used
fictitiously. Any resemblance to actual events, locales or persons, living
or dead is entirely coincidental.*
ISBN: *978-1-938595-00-4*

For My Father

"And the day came when the risk to remain tight in a bud was more painful than the risk it took to blossom."

Anais Nin

From the Desk of Andrea Thane

May 26, 2013

To Ms. Lara Leeds:

You don't know me, but you'll recognize the name on my letterhead. Surprised? Ha! I guess you've grown accustomed to unusual behavior by now. And of course, so have I.

Unless you thought you were Sam's first?

He might have liked giving you that impression. I can see my husband now, approaching your office cubicle, lanky and long-legged in his business suit, silk tie knotted at his throat. He places a large hand on your desktop and leans forward, blue eyes sparkling, cheeks flushed, flying high on his drug of choice: adrenalin.

Nothing beats landing a big account, Sam says. *Couldn't have done it without you.*

Waiting for your smile, Sam's eyes seem serene, the color of a cloudless sky. His jaw is stubbled; it's after five when the beard he combats regains lost territory, but you probably think his shadowed jaw is sexy. Those fine prickly hairs on Sam's urban-pale skin offset his pin-striped suit; the burgeoning beard jazzes up his face, adds a bad boy patina.

So, Lara Leeds, you can't help but smile as your boss— your handsome, bad boy boss—leans close to compliment your work. Then, as your lips curve, the boss's own well-formed mouth breaks into a conspiratorial grin. A tiny warmth flares in your chest, maybe a warning tingle too.

Celebrate with me, Sam Thane says. A single lock of his close-cropped, black hair falls into a half-curl on his forehead.

You stiffen in your swivel chair, but he urges, *Come on.* His claret grin goes crooked. *I'm heading for Jack's Bar.* He gestures in that general direction. *Don't you deserve to celebrate too?*

And you do deserve something, you find yourself thinking. Aren't the graphs you prepared for Sam Thane's latest presentation virtual works of art? Haven't you spent tedious hours at your computer screen inputting data for Thane PR's extensive comparison charts? Don't you deserve some of the boss's energy, some of that easy effervescence bubbling over your desk?

Champagne? He offers, and that settles it.

And, Lara, champagne is all you share that first time, champagne and a touch or two. Yes, Sam's big hands feel warm on your shoulders when he helps with your coat. And straightening your collar there's a second, slower touch.

Now, you're not stupid, my little friend. You notice the boss's hand hovering near your jaw; you feel the backs of his fingers graze your chin. But you don't move away. Not while Sam's cerulean eyes hold yours, not while he murmurs—as though you're not meant to hear, as though he can't stop the words from flowing—*I've never felt so drawn.* Then his sky eyes widen, running over your face, as if you're a miracle, as if he's transported by awe.

Later, Lara, you may wonder about that gaze, those words—what they promise, if anything. But while Sam talks, you are filled with light; I know. His eyes intoxicate; his touch is tender as a prayer. The full force of his attention is an addictive drug, a religion that delivers salvation in the now. Over the next

2

few weeks your stolen hours together grow sacred, set apart from ordinary time. At work, your boring routines are infused with desire. Secrets swell your chest; deep down inside you feel special.

Between visits to Sam's clandestine apartment, you cherish that special sense. Oh, you thought I didn't know about the lavish lair on 40th Street and Second? The boss's custom-designed, fully-equipped, one bedroom hideaway—conveniently located near your midtown office—has been up and running for years. Lara, you're not the first woman (secretary, assistant, junior account executive) to walk across the plush bedroom carpet, letting the finest charcoal gray wool caress the soles of your bare feet.

No, Ms. L.L. (does anyone call you Lala?), you're not the first to lie beside Sam on his fabulous possum fur bedcover or take a soaking bubble bath in his big, black circular tub. I taught him about Occitane; do you like it? A superior product, Occitane makes the water foam with bubbles that don't dissolve but last, so Sam can mold the glistening white froth into snowballs. The first wet fluff gets smoothed over your shoulders; perhaps he kisses your neck. Next, he tongues each of your nipples, gives one a gentle bite.

Does Sam ask you to extend one leg out of the water, draping your knee over the black marble, and letting your calf hang outside the tub? Does he form a fragrant, white, light-as-air mound and froth your dangling foot? I can see him tickling your instep, spreading foam up the back of your calf and into the crease behind your knee. Next his long fingers slide down your thigh, sloping into the tub. His hand dips below the waterline, seeks your most vulnerable, open flesh, finds your hidden layers, blooming and submerged.

Has he shaved you yet, Lara? Sam loves the little girl look, the innocent pubis, smooth and bare. Do you find the exposure thrilling? Or do you sometimes wonder if you've become too vulnerable—your grown woman's sex lips stripped defenseless, rendering the sensitive, salmon-pink tissue more accessible to Sam's strong tongue, his dancing fingers, his thick purple cock? I'm certain Sam's shaved you himself by now; he likes to take control. I can see you sitting on the circumference of his black marble tub, sipping the Cristal he orders by the case.

He spreads your thighs; light jazz plays in the bathroom. It takes trust to let a man approach your nether parts with a straight razor, doesn't it, Lara Leeds? His single blade flicks open like a switch blade, but a little risk is part of the fun, and the Cristal relaxes you, right?

There, just a bit wider, my darling, open up your legs.

You already know Sam's touch is gentle, his fingers nimble and firm. On his fingertips comes a tiny puff of foam—shaving cream. How tenderly he paints it on your pussy.

I know what I'm doing, he promises, before scraping your skin with the blade.

And he does know what he's doing; doesn't he? Sam's tone is persuasive, and his fingers are talented so you spread wide to let him get close, straight blade in hand. You obey instructions, shift positions so he doesn't nick your sensitive skin but sheers your pussy bald. Then, spreading a plush black towel on the dry tub floor, Sam directs you onto your knees.

Bend over; he gestures your face forward, forehead to the towel. *Lift;* his hand guides your buttocks up. *Spread;* he shows you how to pull your cheeks apart, baring the fine fuzzy hairs in the crease. Then, kissing your tailbone, palming the rounds of your butt cheeks, he waits a long moment before raising the straight razor to shave every hair from slit to anus.

Later, when your pubis itches, the discomfort reminds you of Sam, making the itch poignant, a souvenir of your time together. It's comforting to have tangible proof Sam Thane cares about you. Too often your boss is busy, hurrying past your desk with a wave and a wink instead of inviting you to his apartment.

4

Doesn't it drive you crazy that he keeps no routine? It's clever though, you must admit. No way to get complacent. Each time Sam invites you, it's a gift; there's no taking him for granted. But ever wonder, Ms. L.L., why the boss is playing with you? You're not the most poised or striking, not the obvious pick of the lot. Yes, I've passed your office cubicle; even though you are new at Thane PR, I've seen your face, and learned many useful things. For example, you have long black hair. Sam must love to brush it.

Lara, when my husband brushes your fine, straight hair, do you ever think of me? I hope you don't pity me, my little friend. Sam's taken his brush to better locks than yours, to gold and auburn tresses. He always grooms his women, smooths lotion onto their flanks, combs through their manes. He hand-feeds you strawberries dipped in chocolate, doesn't he? Along with tangy seedless grapes. Cubes of cheddar cheese he pops into your mouth, and off his fingers, your tongue licks organic peanut butter from the health food store.

Sam Thane has you in training; I can see it now. He makes you lie down on the possum fur bedspread, takes off all your clothes. Then, standing up, looking down, loosening his tie—he's still in his business suit—he says, *Touch yourself.*

What? you ask the first time.

Touch yourself.

Poor Lara, you're flustered now. Did you know that turns Sam on? He likes that you're awkward, insecure, easily controlled. Yes, you are your boss's type: self conscious and young, unaware of your strengths, malleable and eager.

Masturbate. His tone is hard. And although you're naked—lying on a married man's fur bedspread in his clandestine apartment—the word comes as a shock. *Do it,* a hiss from the handsome mouth that's tongued every inch of your skin.

Reluctantly, you bring your hand to where your sex is naked as a five-year-old's. You slither a finger near your slit and let your eyes slip shut.

Open your eyes. Sam's voice is raw. *Look at me.*

Do you say *I can't*, but open anyway? Do my husband's sky blue orbs pierce your chest, pin you to the bed?

Move your finger. Touch yourself. I want to see you do it.

Eventually, under Sam's relentless gaze, you comply. Eyes open, pubis stripped, finger circling your clit, you let him stand over you, fully clothed, watching. And when you finally surrender, you discover you love the exposure. You love the terror of being seen and the unconditional acceptance of the seer. You love his commands because they relieve your timid soul's fear of failure. Follow Sam's orders, and you will always be right. You will be groomed and fed, adored and petted. Don't you love the attention?

And doesn't it hurt when that attention withdraws, when Sam's sparkling eyes move off? When your boss leaves town for business or pleasure, when he doesn't call over the weekend, when you find yourself wondering about me . . .

Lara, this Tuesday evening, June 1, I'll be at Vincent's Café. Corner of 23rd and Third, 6 PM. Will you come?

Andrea Thane

6

LARA

June 2, 2013

Dear Andrea,

I've started this letter three times before, only to toss it—crumpled—into the garbage. Will my fourth attempt reach a mailbox? Who knows? Yesterday you surprised me so much; I still can't figure out how I feel.

Honestly, I'm not sure what I expected walking into Vincent's Cafe. Your letter scared me, but I confess it also made me crazy curious. Sometimes I still feel like the teenager I was five years ago—a moth drawn to the flame. But I couldn't pass up the opportunity to meet *you*, fluttery creature that I am!

Could you tell I was nervous entering the café? I tried hard to look calm. Your moon round face seemed unspeakably composed, but your green eyes narrowed on me. What were you thinking as you sat straight-backed in your black silk shift, your blond hair billowing around your bare shoulders? From where I stood, you looked like an avenging angel at that corner table with your open bottle of red wine.

Honestly, I didn't know whether to fear or admire you. Didn't know how I was supposed to respond to your broad, pale shoulders, your ivory chest—exposed by that low-cut summer dress. And how tall are you—five foot nine or ten? When you rose, you towered over me despite my three inch heels. I confess, I both disliked and respected you for not bothering to fake a smile.

Yesterday, you were the queen of calculated sophistication, offering your gold-ringed, French-manicured hand over the red-checkered tablecloth. But I wasn't fooled by your civilized veneer. Did you notice the tremble in my grip? An instinctive response to your flesh. Yet I held my ground while we shook hands—in spite of your unveiled intensity, your obvious prowess of a lioness.

It wasn't easy meeting you, but of course I'll understand if you don't think my struggles merit much sympathy. Just don't mock me for being open. Instead, give me one of your indulgent laughs, that low, throaty chuckle I heard yesterday for the first time. Be unpredictable and surprise me again. The way you did during our two hours at Vincent's Café—over and over—the pleasure of it shimmering in your Nordic face until I couldn't hate you anymore, until I found myself hoping that—somehow—you might stop hating me too.

Andy—I still feel funny calling you that, although you say I must—I can easily state I've never met anyone like you. Now, you probably want to scold me for uttering a soupy cliché. You haven't the patience for flattery; you've already told me in no uncertain terms. I worry as I write about doing one of the many things that aggravate or bore you: empty chit chat—I hope I'm not chatting now—lies, white or black, including exaggerations, accidental distortions, and—especially—self delusions.

Well, I won't fall prey to that last mistake. No self deluding here. "Not the most poised or striking" was how you put it in your letter. It hurt me to read that, but I know it's true. Yesterday, I saw myself through your penetrating eyes: a skinny, dark-haired, English Lit major from a town you never heard of upstate. Obvious, right? Who else could I be if not a wannabe, a stupid cliché, dreaming of writing the great American novel, doing grunt work at a PR firm instead?

How I hated watching your coral lips assess my life in a sentence. Sizing me up was a parlor game, but your pale luminous face only reflected a truth I already knew. Yes, there are zillions of small town girls trying to make it in the Big Apple. I hate being ordinary, a dime a dozen, but you wouldn't know how that feels. Life is different for people like you, who write daring letters and dictate their own terms.

Consider this: without explanation or excuse, you invited me to Vincent's Café. Then, serenely lacking self consciousness, you directed me into a chair *beside* you, instead of across the table. What could it mean? I wondered, sinking into the seat that placed my bare shoulder near yours. When you filled my glass with red wine and patted my hand on the tabletop, I felt stunned. Compassion, wasn't it? The last thing I expected.

I have to admire your *sang froid*, the way you gracefully conducted our encounter. Your dignity seemed made of steel, but mine felt much more fragile. "Samuel Trevor Thane," you tossed that moniker out onto our checkered tablecloth, and at first I was startled. A moment later I couldn't help feeling you were right: his full name needed to be spoken between us. Then your glossy lips twitched to avoid a smile, and I saw you enjoyed my discomfort.

Perhaps you can understand why I turned away from you to stare into my wine. Blurting out, "What do you want?" came naturally, but I still don't know how to interpret your simple, unfathomable answer: "To know you." Yesterday, one syllable was all I could manage in reply; the ubiquitous, obnoxious "why?" almost stuck in my throat. Thanks for responding to that with your first smile—a small, sly one. The rest of your answer jolted my chest. I'm still puzzling over what you meant by, "Can't you guess what I want?" Feel free to expound anytime.

Andy, more than once yesterday, you made me feel like a child. Remember when you murmured something about "wanting to be on my side?" I almost let out a sigh of relief, while you took a slow sip of wine. But your next bomb dropped only seconds later: "Sam's difficult," you said.

Those two words sent me flying back to the 40th Street apartment. My last time there Sam's caresses had mixed with his scowls, and he'd barked commands each time I hesitated. Sam—how awkward I feel writing his name, and the words "your husband" feel even worse, redolent of the red letter A that seemed to have emblazoned itself on my forehead as I entered Vincent's Café.

Obviously, I couldn't complain about losing the previously velvet, coaxing voice that had turned rough as sandpaper. Not while *you* sat beside me, pale and broad-shouldered, a stalwart Viking with steady, gem-green eyes and flowing flaxen hair. Quietly, I searched my memory for clues to Sam's attitude change, but your next question gave me a hint. "How long has it been?" Neither of us seemed happy when I admitted to three months. Your level voice remarked, "It doesn't take long for Sam to get difficult," and I had to stifle a sob.

When you claimed you could make me stronger, I wanted to believe you. That's why I let you top off my wine and order those extra hors d'oeurves. But I couldn't cooperate when you said, "Tell me what he does." My lips just burned with shame.

You laughed as I stammered—a low, throaty chuckle that reverberated around us like a loose embrace. Then I found the courage to ask why you're with Sam, but I should have been prepared for your obvious comeback, delivered with a dangerous smile: "Why are you with him?"

I hated myself for stuttering, "I-I don't know." Then, when the word "liar" bubbled out of your mouth and floated between us until it popped, almost audibly, I actually felt relieved. As our food arrived, I wondered if we were drawn to Sam Thane for the same reason. But Andy— with your Viking stature, your flaxen hair and lioness laughter—how could your cravings resemble mine?

Then I remembered your strange letter with its many accurate details. You knew about the commands issued over the possum fur bedspread, the black marble tub and being shaved. Did my face go white as I asked about that? I confess, I held my breath while you calmly dipped calamari in marinara sauce and extended it toward me.

When, at last, you said, "You can't know what you don't experience," I was able to exhale. Then I tried to regain my equilibrium while your gold-ringed hand jiggled calamari in front of me until a red teardrop fell onto the tablecloth, splotching a clean white square.

Andy, was that bright stain an accident? Or did you deliberately shed a single red tear?

Your pinky grazed my lower lip when I finally opened my mouth to let you put the food in. Did you know that? Afterwards, you brought your attention to the mozzarella and tomato, but my lip still felt your finger. What kind of impulse made you urge me to eat? I didn't have the strength to argue when your fork speared a slice of mozzarella and brought it up to my mouth.

I almost gagged on that bland, spongy cheese but, under your cool, grass-green gaze, I forced my teeth to bite through the slab. A moment later I was caught off guard when you twirled that cheese in the air, displaying a cookie cut-out shape of my mouth. Then I watched in amazement as you brought the mozzarella to your lips, licked at the slab as though it were a lollipop, and tongued the tiny indents from my teeth.

I tried to maintain a poker face while draining the rest of my wine. By then I was getting tipsy and probably would've stayed at Vincent's Café, letting you feed (and bait) me all night. But when you glanced at your watch and revealed you had another engagement, I felt a strange mix of relief and disappointment.

Andy, I hope this letter hasn't bothered or bored you too much. I know it might be presumptuous, and I'm not even sure what to hope for. Probably I'm just a naïve young woman, acting on impulse as I too often do.

Yours truly,
Lara Leeds

Date: 6/04/2013   3:42 PM
From: *AndreaThane@gmail.com*
To: *LLeeds@ThanePR.com*
Subject: Hamilton Club

Hello Lara,

I found your note quite charming, in its own way. Not the least bit presumptuous. A real letter is a nice surprise; I so rarely receive one. As a child, I had several pen pals.

Your quaint blow-by-blow analysis of our cocktail hour was quite amusing. "The prowess of a lioness—" I do so enjoy your characterizations of me! But Lara, beware of thinking too highly of others; it only leads to disappointment.

Besides, we are peers, despite my few years more experience. We are practically colleagues in terms of certain matters that I believe interest us both. And in pursuance of those interests, I propose another rendezvous: Tuesday, lunch, 1 PM at the Hamilton Club, 63rd and Park Avenue.

Andrea

Subject: checking in
Date: 6/07/2013   2:58 PM
From: *SThane@ThanePR.com*
To: *AndreaThane@gmail.com*

Darling Andy,

Arrived here in Tokyo 2 days ago. The extra stop in Hong Kong, cementing Thane PR's relationship with Ming Jewels, was worth the effort.

But, as usual, after 48 hrs in Tokyo, I'm ready to come home. Business trips to Asia suck, except for the exotic women, ha, ha. Only kidding, my love. Nothing but the exclusive right to promote Makashi's clothing line to the US market could induce me to spend so long without you. However, I'm determined to remain in Tokyo until a contract is signed—at least a provisional one.

Darling, can you do me a favor? There's an important file on my night table in a navy folder marked "M." Could you drop that by the office? I know Beth would love to see you. If not, contact her and she'll send a messenger to pick it up from the doorman. Wish me luck courting the dour Mr. Makashi.

Love always,

Samuel H. Thane | President
THANE PR INC.
117 Times Square, 3rd Floor, New York, NY 10036
☎direct phone (212) 555-0842
www.ThanePR.com

Subject: checking back
Date: 6/07/2013   6:45 PM
From: *AndreaThane@gmail.com*
To: *SThane@ThanePR.com*

Sam dear,

How sweet of you to be homesick. Don't tell me you're lonely—accompanied by your blond account assistant and bevy of Asian ladies. Only kidding, my dear; luckily, we share the same sense of humor. No problem dropping off your file, and of course, I'll say hi to Beth. If only she were a little less emotional, I'd stop by more often.

Things at home are moving slowly but surely. I'm supervising the contractors in our kitchen as best I can. Leave it to you to coordinate a long business trip with a messy construction job at home! I have half a mind to take a room at the Hamilton Club until the worst is over.

Good luck with Mr. Makashi, my dear, not that you need it. Just turn on the famous Sam Thane charm.

Love, Andy

Subject: Makashi update
Date: 6/07/2013   6:20 PM
From: *SThane@ThanePR.com*
To: *BBlain@ThanePR.com*

Beth, it's slow here, but the outlook is positive. Tomorrow, I view a factory with production in process. There are still a few disagreements over fabric. Delays could forfeit the fall shows. But if necessary, we'll postpone to winter holidays.

Keep an eye on Lara for me. But take it easy on her— whatever you may think about my lifestyle. You're the only one I trust, the only one who's been with Thane PR since the old days.

A last request: will you please check in on Andy? She needs help with an upcoming fund raiser, but she'll never ask.

Thanks in advance

Samuel H. Thane | President
THANE PR INC.
117 Times Square, 3rd Floor, New York, NY 10036
☎direct phone (212) 555-0842
www.ThanePR.com

Subject: Hamilton Club
Date: 6/08/2013 3:53 PM
From: *LLeeds@ThanePR.com*
To: *AndreaThane@gmail.com*

Dear Andy,

All I can say is: wow! I just got back to the office, after spending a too long lunch "hour" with you. Beth Blain—who watches me closely—just chewed me out, but I'm unrepentant. In fact, here I am again, pursuing non-work related issues on company time. But I must write to you, Andy; it simply can't be helped.

Before today, I'd never been in one of those private clubs. Just entering that cool, dark lobby was intimidating on a sunny June day. And, oh my God, that snobby attendant— she swooped down the moment I walked in, asking who'd invited *me*. Clearly, I didn't look like I belonged. Andy, thank heaven you were waiting right there to legitimize me. And thanks for linking your arm in mine as though we were old friends.

It's a good thing I was dressed for work because my jeans wouldn't have made it past the front door. That aggressive lobby attendant would have shooed me right out. Did you catch the dirty look she shot my black linen shift? I guess moneyed Manhattan ladies don't dress like me. You stood out in your ankle-length, turquoise, silk dress. That shimmering sheath flowed down your body like water, and then parted neatly, like the Red Sea, each time you stepped forward with your right leg. When the pale, smooth skin of that long, bare limb became visible—as the side slit opened to mid thigh—I had to suppress a schoolgirl giggle at the grim expression on the lobby attendant's face.

Andy, even if you tried, you couldn't look properly dowdy like those women in pearl necklaces, pastel twin sets, and flowered, below-the-knee length skirts. You stood out more today than at Vincent's, where there was a hodgepodge of types. At the Hamilton Club, you alone exhibited sensuality, moving with animal grace. You were the only woman without hosiery, despite the sweltering summer heat. Of course, it was cool in the air conditioned brownstone. In fact, when we entered the dining room, my skin began to goose bump in my sleeveless dress.

Thanks for removing your crocheted shawl—over my lame protests—and gently wrapping it around my shoulders. I appreciated that your hands refused to hurry even though the maître d' stood before us, working his pursed mouth with impatience. Andy, would it be too weird to say I like the quality of your touch? Yes, it was the *care* your fingers took while adjusting the loose-knit across my back and shoulders, almost like a mother helping her child. It suddenly seems a shame you don't have children; Andy, your touch is so light.

Oh, what nonsense I've been scribbling—the habit of free associating on paper acquired over years of journal keeping. Can you forgive my unruly thoughts flowing onto these pages? If I'm too boring, you can skim. Or perhaps I'll learn to control myself, give you headlines only. For example: **Office Worker Shocked by Elegant Dining Room**. Honestly, Andy, I've never seen a restaurant—even in a fancy hotel—with so much space between the tables. Wasn't our white-clothed circle a miniature world, complete with oversized, silver-plated cutlery, individual crystal salt and pepper shakers, and fresh-cut flowers? This time when you directed the maître d' to seat us side by side—he pulled out both our chairs—I knew better than to be surprised. I've decided it's cozier sitting next-to rather than across-from; Andy, I like your style.

The Caesar's salad was a great recommendation; I enjoyed the table-side show. It's old hat for you, I suppose, but I felt like I'd walked into an old fashioned, European novel when the bow-tied waiter rolled over a cart with salad ingredients and bowed. All this formality in the middle of a boiling hot summer day made me want to giggle. Not that you could tell time or temperature inside that dining room, where we were hermetically sealed.

Did you realize I nearly embarrassed us both when you tapped my hand and tipped your blond head toward the table to our right? You didn't have to explain why you wanted me to look. The identically outfitted mother–daughter team was a caricature of itself. I was happy you felt close enough to share an inside joke with me. At least, Andy, I felt "inside." Am I?

I guess that brings me to my next question. The real reason for this email. Although I appreciate that you said I don't need a reason to write you, and I'm pleased to provide entertainment, nevertheless . . . nevertheless . . I must summon my nerve to face you, even over the Internet. Although I don't have to watch your face, I struggle to put down the words: <u>why me?</u> Why me for this bounty of attention? Why me for this great flattery? Why the girl you're supposed to hate, the one who's been sleeping with your husband?

Yes, I'm sitting here wondering why, when I said my neck hurt, you cared enough to rise from your seat and stand behind me, using your hands to soothe my pain. Andy, where did you learn to press like a masseuse? Your strong fingers massaged my shoulders as though you were

21

licensed by the Swedish Institute. For all I know, you are. It certainly seemed like you knew what to do when your hands moved beneath my hair, up the back of my neck. Then, when your fingers pressed the base of my skull, kneading the tiny knots near the top of my spine, it was heaven. But next you bent down and whispered into my ear two phrases I still don't understand. "Let me," you said. And moments later, "Let go." After that I could have sworn something soft and wet brushed my neck, but I'm sure it was an illusion.

Incredibly, after that we ate our lunches and spoke of movies and museums, as if nothing unusual had happened. That ordinary talk was calming, but when you couldn't believe I'd never been to the Frick Museum, I found myself squirming in my chair, feeling a bit like your wayward protégé. Honestly, I don't know how to interpret what's happening between us, or even what I'm looking to convey in this letter. But it's certainly true that—in the polite quiet of the Hamilton Club dining room, surrounded by chintz, Liberty prints, and framed oil paintings of dogs—you once again differed dramatically from my expectations. I'll close with thanks for a lovely lunch and hope that my foolishness has, at least, entertained you.

Lara

Lara Leeds | Administrative Assistant
THANE PR INC.
117 Times Square, 3rd Floor, New York, NY 10036
☎direct phone (212) 555-0843
www.ThanePR.com

Robin Reinach

Hand delivered to the reception desk at Thane PR

From the Desk of Andrea Thane

June 10, 2013

Dear Lara,

Is it so surprising I enjoy your company? Granted, we met in an unusual way, but we're unusual people. Here's something to think about: many woman in your situation wouldn't have shown up at Vincent's Cafe that first day. Yet you insist on underestimating yourself, ignoring your courage, discrediting your candor and adventurous spirit. Don't be one of those young women who undervalue their gifts; make the most of them instead.

For example, you have symmetrical features, a doll-like mouth. Why don't you line your brown eyes with kohl? The effect would be striking, especially if your lips went wine-red. Lara, why not acknowledge and improve your strengths? If I were your fairy godmother, I'd wave my wand until you trusted your lithe body and your curious mind to follow their instincts and intuitive flashes. However, my magic wand is out of order, so we'll have to pursue your education in slower ways. A visit to the Frick is mandatory; this Saturday morning at eleven o'clock your tutor will be in front of the museum.

Andy

Subject: Hamilton Club
Date: 6/10/2013   6:02 PM
From: *AndreaThane@gmail.com*
To: *SThane@ThanePR.com*

Sam dear,

I'm taking a room at the Hamilton, but will stop by the apartment every day. Our contractor still claims to be on schedule and promises a sleek result. However, I can't live with all the noise and dust. Tell me, has the famously difficult Makashi succumbed to your courtship yet? If not, I'd push forward that blond account executive. Linda's the one you traveled with, right? Perhaps you've already thought of that, my dear. In fact, that may even be the reason you brought her along. (A small, dark-haired woman, for example, wouldn't be as exotic to an Asian as a blond.) I'm sure you remember how Mr. Makashi stared at me last month when we took him out to dinner. If you haven't already, let the blonde get close to him. That is, if she's not close to you.

On a brighter note, when I dropped off your file, Beth insisted on helping with the fund raiser. I know you put her up to it, Sam, and that was actually very sweet. I had a last minute screw up with a favor supplier over rainbow pens, but Beth found someone to rush my order, so thanks. Sam dear, are you still planning to return on schedule and attend the event yourself? That's the help I appreciate most. After all this time, I still like to see your face in the audience. As there are extra tickets, I invited Beth to the SK gala.

Love, Andy

Subject: Fund Raiser
Date: 6/11/2013   8:06 PM
From: *SThane@ThanePR.com*
To: *AndreaThane@gmail.com*

Darling Andy,

I'll be sitting in the front row when you deliver your speech. The work you do with SK is for both of us. Thanks for dropping off my file and inviting Beth to the gala—long time since we've treated her to anything outside the office.

As to your savvy suggestion, Linda is already hovering around Makashi, anticipating his every wish. (Maybe not *every* wish. You do know she's married?) I hate to predict an outcome before I'm certain, but you know I'd never have flown all the way to Japan, and stayed here for this length of time, if I hadn't thought we had a damn good shot at Makashi, Inc.

Enjoy the Hamilton, my darling. Why don't you get a massage while you're there? Or a mud wrap. You haven't said you missed me, but I hope you do. Every time I eat shrimp tempura I think of you.

Love, Sam

Samuel H. Thane | President
THANE PR INC.
117 Times Square, 3rd Floor, New York, NY 10036
☎direct phone (212) 555-0842
www.ThanePR.com

Delivered by FedEx on 6/11/2013

PEARL OF THE ORIENT NOVELTIES
TOKYO, HONK KONG

Dear Lara,

Do you miss me? Maybe this gift will help. For obvious reasons—I never tried Ben Wa balls myself, but I hear they give great pleasure. Asian ladies have enjoyed them for centuries. Naturally, I couldn't let you go deprived.

You'll see two gold balls on a string; simply insert them, while allowing the string to hang out for handy removal. (A gentle tugging on the dangling string may also feel quite nice.) The saleslady told me the balls won't fall out, just as tampons don't. But you would know more about that.

One warning, my sweet: don't wear them into a store with a detector device at the entrance. The saleslady warned me that Ben Wa balls occasionally set off the alarm. I have to admit I got a kick out of picturing you in that scene.

I await a full description of your Ben Wa experience, my sweet. You have a talent for verbalizing the erotic, and I crave your sexy voice.

Love,

Sam

Subject: your gift arrived
Date: 6/11/2013   4:08 PM
From: *LLeeds@ThanePR.com*
To: *SThane@ThanePR.com*

Sam, thanks for the (uh, unique, creative, downright weird?) gift. I won't use it shopping, that's for sure. I'll experiment at home, trying not to think too much about what *you're* doing for entertainment. I know how your long fingers, nimble tongue, and hard cock hate to stay idle.

There's a taste of my dirty talk that you claim to miss. You could always call, Sam, if you wanted to hear my voice. I can waft sweet nothings across oceans of phone wire until they land in your lap. Or text me again, as if we were high school kids.

Think of me, all alone in New York with nothing to console me but some weird balls on a string.

xxx Lara

Lara Leeds | Administrative Assistant
THANE PR INC.
117 Times Square, 3rd Floor, New York, NY 10036
☎direct phone (212) 555-0843
www.ThanePR.com

Subject: Henry Altman
Date: 6/13/2013   10:47 PM
From: *LLeeds@ThanePR.com*
To: *AndreaThane@gmail.com*

Dear Andy,

Once again our time together turned out so differently from the way I'd imagined. Of all people from my past, I never expected to encounter Henry Altman from Ann Arbor, Michigan at the Frick Museum! And in the Fragonard Room—where I was feeling so cultured and mature—discussing "The Progress of Love" in erudite tones, enjoying the romantic whimsy of Fragonard as if it were a regular topic of conversation for me.

No doubt I was feeling too high and mighty (a side effect of being near *you*). Life had to send me a reminder—a blast from the past to make me feel vulnerable. "Fly close to the sun, and you will get burned," my mother used to say when I longed to run with the popular crowd and crushed on the cutest guys. Andy, if my mother had seen me at the Frick, with the kohl lining my eyes, wearing that frilly white sundress and surrounded by huge, exquisitely-detailed oil paintings, she'd have thought I was flying pretty high.

Yes, I'd soared higher than Mom would have thought healthy, and my mood was in sync with the room we occupied—light and airy, hushed and elegant. I wasn't manic the way I sometimes get when trying to act sophisticated. Instead I felt centered, well-bred and spirited, like a lady from one of Fragonard's paintings. That cotton eyelet sundress helped, giving me a stylish, but old fashioned feel. Clad entirely in white, with the bodice hugging my waist as tight as a corset, and all those flounces and ruffles at the bottom of my skirt, how could I fail to feel special?

But special doesn't suit me, no matter how much I wish it did. That's why fate interrupted my flight at the Frick to penetrate my façade. Yes, I'm too easily subject to floods of unwelcome emotion. Probably, that kind of thing doesn't happen to you? But I don't want to idealize; you've warned me against that already. And perhaps, as you said later, 24 is a self conscious age.

Andy, here's where I pause, sucking my lower lip, tapping my finger on the keyboard. I'm sitting in bed with my laptop . . . stalling.

Deep breath.

Let me begin by admitting what I'm sure you've already guessed: Henry was—briefly—my lover.

Andy, I'm not surprised you didn't approve of his style. That slight curl of your upper lip told me everything—your subtle coral sneer. Henry's sandy blond beard and longish hair were too casual for you, right? And his lopsided grin projected more youthful impertinence than you probably enjoy. With those boyish dimples denting his cheeks and in his faded jeans, Henry Altman still looked like a college kid. Like the Ann Arbor townie he was when I met him, a puppy dog-ish Midwestern intellectual, the son of a mathematics professor at the University of Michigan, where we both were students.

Andy, I saw that Henry's joking, laid-back attitude didn't impress you. His usually infectious chuckle only changed your sneer to a smirk. But he can be serious when he chooses, and he's very smart too. At college, Henry had a

3.8 average, in addition to being a marathon runner, with all the drive and commitment that implies. Under those faded jeans, his legs are muscular. And behind his black-framed glasses lie big, brown eyes. I wonder, could you see the intelligence that hides behind those lenses?

Now, I imagine you're growing impatient because I haven't told you why he made me so nervous. But Andy, you're beginning to understand (aren't you?) why, when I was trying to put my best foot forward, I might be flustered by a reminder of the scruffy kid I used to be. Not so long ago I dressed the way Henry does: in faded jeans and cheap jewelry, like his chunky silver rings. Yes, I caught your ladylike shudder when Henry's hand reached for my cheek, when his fingers flashed that shiny collection and demonstrated their familiarity with my skin.

I saw your gem-green eyes go haughty then, your pale chin lift to jut forward. But, was it because Henry touched me as if he had the right, as if—after three years—there was still a bond between us? Andy, when Henry's arm encircled my back, I sensed something stronger than irritation twisting your glossy pink lips. But maybe I'm reading too much into things.

I bet you don't fret over chance meetings between people from different parts of your life. I wish you *were* my fairy godmother, and a wave of your magic wand could imbue me with confidence like your own. If I feel into your stature—borrow your height and broad shoulders, visualize your shimmering blond mane falling down my back, if I imagine that my eyes are level with men's faces instead of below them looking up—I can almost get a visceral sense of your contained power.

But I can't hold on to it. Gravity sets in; I drop back down, and my personality dissolves into its usual (how did you characterize me in your first letter? Ah, yes "malleable") state. Yes, confidence feels a bit like flying too high, but Andy, I notice the sun's fierce heat doesn't burn *you*. I'm the type who gets singed and seared for overstepping my bounds. You remarked that seeing Henry made me nervous, and you'll soon understand why. But I couldn't have told this story at the Frick Museum, not with strangers milling around and knowing you had to leave soon.

Incidentally, where are you always rushing? These mysterious "prior engagements" that must remain unnamed—are you sure they're not dates? I wouldn't blame you if they were, and it might even help to explain things. Oh, well, your story must wait for another day, I suppose. If I'm ever going to hear it. Mine is slated for now, but you'll forgive my starting slowly.

To begin with, please imagine my senior year at the University of Michigan, or as my college advisor boasted, "The Harvard of the Midwest." I shared a house off campus with seven other students. Henry Altman was our de-facto leader, maybe because he was a local, maybe because he was willing to do the work. At first I thought him too bland, like his voice. Is that an accent or the absence of one? I was never able to decide. Anyway, like so many people from the Midwest, Henry moved and spoke more slowly than we do here in NYC. But he was competent in a matter-of-fact, Midwestern way, collecting funds for expenses and stocking the kitchen with health food.

Henry Altman's room was next to mine, and I often walked in to chat and check out his gadgets. He was an inventor, always tinkering with some new creation, a miniature robot or remote control helicopter. (Henry designed adult items

31

too; comic thingamabobs with light-up buttons, one-of-a kind puzzles, and mechanical gizmos with whirling parts that were displayed on his bookshelves.) Yesterday at the Frick, I was surprised to hear him talk about his "cottage industry success." In college, I never thought he'd make money on that novelty item stuff. Maybe it's the website he set up, the low overhead, selling directly to consumers?

Uh-oh Andy, am I boring you? I didn't mean to beat around the bush. Tell you what, I'll follow your example from our first meeting and toss out a name the way you did at Vincent's Café—Terry Lee Taylor. She was Henry's girlfriend senior year, and she spent a lot of time at our house. Terry Taylor sang ballads and played guitar while Henry fiddled with his inventions. Often I sat transfixed by our shared bedroom wall, listening to her serenade him until one kind of music ended, another began, and the sounds of their lovemaking penetrated the thin layers of plaster and paint that separated them from me.

After school ended in June most of the kids took off, but Henry and I stayed at our house for two extra weeks. Our rent was paid the whole month, and I was in no hurry to move back with my parents. The first night after graduation, I heard Terry singing. Her melody drew me out of my room, down the hall to where Henry's door stood ajar. Stepping quietly toward the threshold, I didn't mean to sneak or spy. I just wanted to see the sweetness of the scene that went with the music—without disturbing it—without interrupting the intimacy radiating from that room.

So I tip-toed to the door and peaked through to find Terry sitting naked on the bed, strumming her guitar. Terry Taylor was slender and small; her long hair was blond, and it rippled—Lady Godiva-like—over her pale shoulders, down her delicate torso till the ends feathered the small of her back. From my angle, with the door half-closed, I couldn't see Henry. I didn't know whether he too was naked, if the couple had just made love or were about to. Terry's acoustic guitar covered the triangle of her sex, but her breasts were visible. Firm and white, they rested on the honey-colored instrument's upper curve, pink nipples protruding.

Still on the threshold, I drew a sharp breath. That was all it took; Terry's attention turned to me. But her light-brown eyes went curious instead of angry, and her tender song continued. Her open gaze held me in place while her eyes asked questions. My prickling flesh sent wordless answers until her lips broke into a smile. Then, still singing, her gaze steady, Terry jerked her chin—an invitation to enter.

"What is it?" Henry's voice came from the other side of the room.

"Lara." She stopped singing, and rose to stand nude, before me.

Frozen in the doorway, I neither walked in nor looked away, but stared straight forward, unable to lower my eyes from the shock of Terry's calm nakedness.

"Lara?" Henry's voice was puzzled; he came into view, wearing only white jockey shorts and glasses. Barefoot, he stood lean and compact; his pale chest was hairless except for a few dirty blond sprigs orbiting nipples too pink for a man.

"S-sorry," I stuttered, finally mobilizing to take a shaky step back.

But Terry swept forward, her pointy white breasts aimed at me, both hands extended.

Andy, I have to stop here. But perhaps I've already said enough? For two timeless weeks I was part of a threesome. It's never happened again. There, that's it. I'm pressing the send button right now before I lose my nerve.

Lara Leeds | Administrative Assistant
THANE PR INC.
117 Times Square, 3rd Floor, New York, NY 10036
☎direct phone (212) 555-0843
www.ThanePR.com

Subject: hi from Lara
Date: 6/13/2013   10:04 PM
From: *LLeeds@ThanePR.com*
To: *HAltman@AltmanGizmo.com*

Henry, what a shock to see you at the Frick! You look the same as ever, but I've changed so much these last three years. BTW, your website is great!

But I'm never one hundred percent sure about those "contact us" buttons, although *yours* probably works, it still feels like my words are sailing off into cyberspace. I just hope they'll float safely toward you.

Hit the reply button, Henry; tell me what's going on in your life. And by the way, who reads incoming mail on this site? Only you, or are there assistants?

Let me know, Lara.

PS. Ever hear from Terry?

Lara Leeds | Administrative Assistant
THANE PR INC.
117 Times Square, 3rd Floor, New York, NY 10036
☎**direct phone (212) 555-0843**
www.ThanePR.com

Delivered by hand to Thane PR

From the Desk of Andrea Thane

June 15, 2013

Dear Lara,

I can't quite say you fulfilled your promise—not with that abrupt cut off just as you were getting to the interesting part. But I did enjoy that tantalizing, if introductory, taste of your initiation into a *ménage a trois*.

Lara, you must know by now that I don't harbor judgments about unconventional sex situations. But I do wish you'd drop your allegiance to your mother's dire prediction. The myth of Icarus, to which her threat refers, is a cautionary tale told by the envious to frighten the daring from reaching too high.

Fate didn't send Henry Altman to melt your wings. Unless I'm mistaken—and I never am about these things—the fellow holds you in great esteem. His eyes, shining with admiration, were unable to leave your face. No, Lara, it wasn't fate or even what you called my "haughty" attitude. I regret having to say that you were the one who turned a chance meeting with your former lover into an awkward experience.

Truly, I had no problem with Henry Altman's "style." Looking young is no crime, and I've always had a soft spot for the gentleman-hippie look. About the sneer you thought you saw, I have no idea. Perhaps I was swallowing or my mouth had an itch. You can't hang on my every tic or twitch, Lara. It just isn't healthy.

Nevertheless, something good has come of this incident, which has inspired me to repeat my offer to make you stronger. I've checked into the Hamilton Club for a few days. (They have some lovely Victorian style rooms here.) And I'd like to invite you to join me at the spa for a whirlpool and sauna. Since I had to stop by the office and pick up some pens from Beth, I decided to leave this note with the receptionist. I know it's short notice, and they've predicted thunderstorms for tomorrow, but perhaps you'll be brave enough to join me anyway, after work. Could you make it by six o'clock? I'll just be finishing my yoga class then.

Lara, I'll leave your name at the front desk in the lobby. Don't let the attendant intimidate you. As you enter the club, square your shoulders; remind yourself you're an invited guest. Pretend to be me, if you must. I find that idea quite amusing, and I'm perfectly willing to loan out my persona, if it helps.

Fondly,

Andy

Subject: checking in
Date: 6/15/2013   1:06 PM
From: *AndreaThane@gmail.com*
To: *SThane@ThanePR.com*

Sam dear,

I'm enjoying the Hamilton and making use of the spa
facilities as you suggested. I'm glad shrimp tempura
reminds you of me, and I hope you're eating a lot of it. Our
kitchen is coming together, but a snafu with the cabinets
near the sink has caused a delay. I'm keeping my room at
the club; you can join me here when you return. Won't that
be romantic?

As to Mr. Makashi, I'm pleased to hear my instincts are still
good, even though it's been ten years since I slaved for you
at Thane PR. How has the blonde fared with him? And
about her being married, when has *that* ever made a
difference to you?

Sam dear, I'm delighted the timing has worked out so you
can attend the fund raiser. In spite of everything, I find
myself looking forward to your return.

Love, Andy

Subject: checking back
Date: 6/16/2013   4:13 AM
From: *SThane@ThanePR.com*
To: *AndreaThane@gmail.com*

Andy darling, I'm happy you miss me—in your own way, of course. And it's my honor to support you at the SK gala. Knowing you, everything's ready, and the event will go down like clockwork. Darling, if your work with SK wasn't so important, I'd try to steal you back. When you left Thane PR, I lost my best right hand. My current assistant can't hold a candle to you.

About the kitchen, I'd like to talk with that contractor myself. Sometimes a man's voice makes things move faster. Although, my love, if any woman can whip a contractor into shape, it's you. As to Makashi, I'm hoping for a happy ending (ha, ha!) Linda (aka "my blond assistant") is doing a bang up job. Pun intended.

Darling, I look forward to kissing your lovely lips. To running my hands over your marvelous big breasts and sucking your nipples till they crinkle erect. When I get home, I swear I'm going to lay you down on the bed and tongue you so slowly you'll cry out for mercy. If you felt like giving me a treat, you could get a Brazilian. See you tomorrow. Love always,

Samuel H. Thane | President
THANE PR INC.
117 Times Square, 3rd Floor, New York, NY 10036
☎direct phone (212) 555-0842
www.ThanePR.com

Subject: work attitude
Date: 6/16/2013 4:17 AM
From: *SThane@ThanePR.com*
To: *LLeeds@ThanePR.com*

Lara, what's going on? Beth says you're acting odd:
distracted, taking long lunch hours, conducting personal
business during office hours. We've already talked about
your taking advantage of our special relationship. Speaking
of which, you haven't emailed me about the Ben Wa balls.
I'm disappointed in you, my sweet. Unless my long absence
has put a damper on your usual alacrity?

Unfortunately, the Makashi deal is going to take longer than
I thought. Makashi is responding to persuasion—finally
looking at the American teen demographic as a market for
his new line. But there's no way to hurry things without
insulting him, and that will kill the deal. I'm flying into
NYC for important business this Thurs., but only staying the
weekend. Then it's back to Tokyo until I get a signed
contract.

Now Lara, I don't want to hear Beth complain about you
anymore. Behave yourself. Be a good girl, and don't give
the office manager so much grief. Or I might have to think
of a way to punish you while I'm in town. (Ha, ha.)

Samuel H. Thane | President
THANE PR INC.
117 Times Square, 3rd Floor, New York, NY 10036
☎direct phone (212) 555-0842
www.ThanePR.com

Subject: work habits
Date: 6/16/2013   7:37 AM
From: *LLeeds@ThanePR.com*
To: *SThane@ThanePR.com*

Come on Sam, you know Beth doesn't like me, and you know why. Don't forget, before you left you promised to protect me from her maternal, middle-aged jealousy. Especially since it's at least half your fault! I swear, you're lucky Beth's in her fifties, or she wouldn't be content as your mother hen.

Now Sam, don't pretend you haven't felt her gaze burning a hole in the back of your dark, curly head. And you must have noticed the way her face goes liquid when you wink a blue eye and flash your famous, wide-mouthed grin.

Sam, you—of all people—know how women are. You know what I'm talking about. Please, believe me; don't make me beg. Other than one longish lunch—on a slow summer day—I didn't do anything wrong. xxx Lara

P.S. If you stop being mad, I'll look forward to seeing you and try the Ben Wa balls.

Lara Leeds | Administrative Assistant
THANE PR INC.
117 Times Square, 3rd Floor, New York, NY 10036
☎direct phone (212) 555-0843
www.ThanePR.com

Subject: Hi Again
Date: 6/16/2013   1:05 PM
From: LLeeds@ThanePR.com
To: HAltman@AltmanGizmo.com

Henry, I'm glad things are going so well for you. Except the part about Terry getting married! But your email said you don't mind? Three years must be longer than I thought.

Thanks for the sweet compliment. No one ever said I looked "exotic" before. Yes, I admit, there <u>was</u> something different about my eyes. So, you're on Fire Island for the summer? I never knew you had a grandfather on the east coast. And he left you a summer house on Fire Island, how great is that? Thanks for the invite. I'd love to visit—later in the season—right now, there's too much going on.

Which brings me to your question: that "older woman" at the Frick Museum was Andrea Thane, a friend. Sort of. Actually, I'm uncertain what's going on with her. But I'm not surprised you picked up "a vibe." Sometimes I think Andy's coming on to me, but—you won't believe this—for the last three months, <u>I've been having an affair with her husband!</u> In my defense, the man's a practiced philanderer. But I've been a bad girl, and I'm trusting you not to hate me for it.

Now Henry, here comes the weirdest part of my little tale: <u>Andrea Thane knows about my affair with her husband.</u> Do you think she's planning to lure me into a dark alley and stab me in the back once she's gained my trust? It would hardly be worth the effort she's made to win me over. Unless she's a true psychopath, like out of a horror movie?

Honestly, sometimes that creepy thought crosses my mind. Do you think it's my conscience, scaring me? Well, there's something even scarier and more confusing—the way I feel about her. Magnetized, *drawn*, like a movie detective who falls in love with the charismatic murderer he's pursuing. You know, I haven't been with a woman since Terry, but I get this sparkly, excited feeling around Andy. You remarked on the outfit I wore to the Frick? That's how she makes me feel—fluttery and girlish, as if I want to wear something so tight it hurts, like that corset-styled top.

Oh God, Henry, why do I crave that woman's attention? By rights, I should have the upper hand in this relationship. (I'm not the one whose husband is cheating.) Yet, around Andy, I feel both elevated and lowered. Lower than *her*, that is.

Henry, I hope you don't mind my being so frank, but we were once intimate in such an unusual way, and you're set safely apart from the rest of my life. Send me your thoughts if you have any, old friend, if you can shed any light on the mystery of my current weird situation.

The force be with you, Lara

Lara Leeds | Administrative Assistant
THANE PR INC.
117 Times Square, 3rd Floor, New York, NY 10036
☎direct phone (212) 555-0843
www.ThanePR.com

Subject: official warning
Date: 6/16/2013 5:22 PM
From: *BBlain@ThanePR.com*
To: *LLeeds@ThanePR.com*
Cc: *SThane@ThanePR.com*

Ms. Leeds:

I stopped by your desk ten minutes ago and specifically stated that I needed you to stay late. Now I see that you've left the office in spite of my request. Let me remind you that your contract with Thane PR specifically includes overtime, within reason, *at the discretion of management.*

Your refusal to work this evening—leaving me here alone to meet our deadline during a terrible thunderstorm—combined with your flustered inability to produce a reasonable excuse, was extremely unprofessional. I regret having to go on record with this official warning. However, I would be remiss in my duties if I did not point out that your conduct this evening was both unprofessional and unacceptable.

Beth Blain

Beth Blaine | Office Manager
THANE PR INC.
117 Times Square, 3rd Floor, New York, NY 10036
☎direct phone (212) 555-0845
www.ThanePR.com

Subject: official warning
Date: 6/17/2013 6:55 AM
From: *SThane@ThanePR.com*
To: *LLeeds@ThanePR.com*

Lara, why am I reading Beth's complaints on my laptop in the airport between flights? I'm tired, I'm rushed, and I'm not in the mood for this. What's going on? And don't give me any more bull about jealousy. Beth needs your support when I'm out of town. It's your job to give it to her.

Besides, you're usually such an eager beaver. Something I've always liked about you, Lara—how hard you try to please. It just isn't like you—rushing out of the office, turning down extra money for overtime. Unless you met someone? Lara, is that the reason you haven't sent an email about my little Ben Wa gift?

I won't share you with another man. No matter what you may think about my situation. You'd better smarten up and give Beth the respect she deserves. Lara, get your act together, and be ready for me tomorrow.

Sam

Samuel H. Thane | President
THANE PR INC.
117 Times Square, 3rd Floor, New York, NY 10036
☎direct phone (212) 555-0842
www.ThanePR.com

Subject: official warning
Date: 6/17/2013   7:34 AM
From: *LLeeds@ThanePR.com*
To: *SThane@ThanePR.com*

Sam, I swear to God there's no other man. And you know I'd never leave Thane PR in the lurch unless I got stuck in a crisis. But I had to meet my old friend, whose fiancé dumped her. She was practically suicidal last night. Sam, I hope you'll forgive my rushing out to rescue an old friend. With all that thunder and lightning, I'd certainly have preferred to stay at the office.

Now I'm pleading with you to honor your promise and help me out with Beth. It was so sweet on our last night together, when—between kisses—you gallantly offered me your protection. I was touched by the way your blue eyes softened, as they so rarely do. You raked your hand through your curly black hair, your dark-red lips formed a genuine smile, and I thought you really meant it.

Please, Sam, don't abandon your fair maiden now, when you're almost home. After all we've been through, can't you take my side this once? I really need you to stand up for me tomorrow.

Love, Lara.

Lara Leeds | Administrative Assistant
THANE PR INC.
117 Times Square, 3rd Floor, New York, NY 10036
☎direct phone (212) 555-0843
www.ThanePR.com

Subject: Thanks for making me laugh!
Date: 6/17/2013 9:20 PM
From: *LLeeds@ThanePR.com*
To: *HAltman@AltmanGizmo.com*

Henry, I've missed your sense of humor, and your insights are dead on. Yes, Andrea Thane is an unusual woman, and as you say, beautiful in an oddly androgynous way. Not only her stature, but something else about her bearing is. . . not masculine exactly, but too strong or matter-of-fact for what I ordinarily think of as feminine. My God, Henry, listen to what I'm saying! Feminists would kill me: I suppose I deserve it.

Still, I'm glad you find my current triangular situation amusing. I was hoping it would be—taken from the right point of view. You wouldn't believe the complications that have already begun to arise. For example: I just had to explain to my boss why I couldn't work overtime yesterday. Obviously, meeting his wife for a spa date at the Hamilton Club wouldn't make a good excuse. Can you imagine?

So I scrambled, typed up this story about having to leave work to help a friend in trouble. Then, sitting at my laptop, getting ready to email my excuse to Japan, it hit me: <u>I have no way of knowing what Andy tells Sam</u>. Now, it doesn't seem likely she'd want him to know we were meeting, but *anything* feels possible with Andrea Thane. And everything seems risky. So I just sat there for a while, fingers paused about the keyboard, trying to parse things out. Finally, I tapped the send button.

I tell you, the whole thing makes me nervous, but I admit it's flattering to be sought after by a husband and wife team—as you so gallantly pointed out. And Henry, how sweet you are, threatening to "jump on the bandwagon." I must agree with your lament: how *did* you let me get away senior year when our lease was over? After those two intimate weeks, I'd have followed you anywhere! But seriously, I always thought you'd move in with Terry. That never happened, huh? Ah, what becomes of the best laid plans and the best laid girls?

Jokes aside, I'd love to come to Fire Island—maybe sometime mid-July? Thanks so much for inviting me. Henry, I can just picture your cute cottage by the sea, with a sandy beach for your backyard. Were you OK during that terrible thunderstorm yesterday?

I almost feel jealous of the gang you're living with this summer, even though I know you only rented out shares to make extra cash. The thought of group living makes me nostalgic for our house senior year, where there was always someone to hang out and watch old movies with. Sometimes I think privacy is overrated; I hate watching videos alone. But you have the perfect balance with the place to yourself Monday through Friday and summer share people on weekends. Leave it to you, Henry, to have your cake and eat it too. You always were resourceful.

So, my old friend, while you're enjoying the sea and the sand, think of me stuck in muggy Manhattan. But don't be too sorry for this lonesome, skyscraper dweller. I've recently been a guest (twice!) at the swanky Hamilton Club, where Andrea Thane is a member.

Did you know there's a full service health spa nestled within the hallowed confines of that aged and genteel brownstone? Well, there is, with a whirlpool and sauna. Since yesterday, when Yours Truly shirked overtime to enjoy the pleasures of that inner sanctum with her new best friend, I haven't been able to think of anything else.

Anyway Henry, I'm glad you have email. I don't know how I survived this long without you in my life. We've got to stay in touch now. Write back and make me laugh again.

Yours, Lara

Lara Leeds | Administrative Assistant
THANE PR INC.
117 Times Square, 3rd Floor, New York, NY 10036
☎direct phone (212) 555-0843
www.ThanePR.com

Journal—June 17, 2013

At the Hamilton Club—I began outside looking in, peering through a glass door at the tall and fabulous, flaxen-haired Andrea Thane finishing her yoga class. Andrea's broad, toned back was toward me; a mirrored wall reflected her bare arms and long legs in their light-blue tights. As she stretched into the last few postures, my eyes ran up her flat stomach to where her skimpy sky-blue workout top clung to her breasts, molding her pointy nipples.

There Andy emerged from the classroom, her skin glistening, her cheeks flushed. Her chest was shiny with a thin film of sweat; the flimsy workout top had gone transparent, glued to her skin. Her palm felt warm as it landed—ever so casually—on my upper back. She kissed both my cheeks, European style.

I felt self-conscious in my sleeveless, tomato-red dress as A's gem-green eyes grazed my chest, stomach, thighs. Then she took my hand—hers was moist from exercise—and led me to the ladies' changing room. There she peeled off her damp yoga gear, while indicating an open, full-length locker for the clothes I wouldn't need in the whirlpool and sauna.

As Andy regarded me unabashedly, I found it difficult to undress. Her own scant outfit was off in a second, but I dawdled with my zipper, shooting furtive glances at her big breasts and curving hips. I pretended interest in the bathrobe that hung in my locker, but I felt like a weird, low-life criminal, unable to stop my eyes from darting sideways to the cleft between Andrea's thighs.

Her blond thatch was shaved slender; the pale flesh of her vulva, like an upside down tulip, was visible on either side of that narrow light-blond strip. Yet—at a quick glance anyway— Andy's sex didn't look exposed the way mine feels after shaving. In fact, her petal-like parts looked

sturdy enough to command respect, like a painting by
Georgia O'Keeffe.

Andrea had donned her terrycloth robe by the time I
stepped out of my clothing. She watched me from a chaise
while her hands expertly twisted her hair into a knot on top
of her head. The bemused expression on her face could
have been mistaken for daydreaming, but I felt those
emerald eyes burn down the front of my body to land,
searing, on the pubis her own husband had shaved bare.

I had prepared for that ruthless gaze by removing
the stubbles that had grown back. But I found myself
unable to breathe until at last my robe hugged my
shoulders and was belted around my waist. That protection
lasted only as long as it took Andy to lead me to the circular
whirlpool, where three naked women were already
submerged. Then Andrea shed her robe and stepped into
the swirling water.

Her back was straight, her neck long and regal.
There was none of my usual squealing or moaning, just a
steady, slow walk into the steaming tub. Sinking gracefully
onto the underwater bench, she let the whirlpool flow over
her shoulders. A few wisps of flaxen hair came loose at
Andy's temples as she beckoned to me. The hot tub ladies
talked among themselves, but I felt their attention on me
sharpen.

In spite of that, I un-sashed my robe, letting it fall
open. Andrea stared at me frankly as the warm, wet air hit
my skin, but the others slid sly glances at my shorn pubis.
I'd have given anything for the proverbial fig leaf; even a g-
string would have offered some protection. But I had
nothing. I was suddenly a girl among women, a working
class lass stripped bare before the aristocracy, a
submissive waiting for dominants to determine her value.
For several terrible moments, I stood like that—my robe
hanging open, my thighs pressed together—my private

parts, smooth as those of a pre-pubescent child, on merciless display.

Finally Andy tilted her chin at a brass hook on the wall, and I hung my robe with all the dignity I could muster. Then I stepped forward, feeling my breasts firm and high, letting my lean thighs and curved calves carry me across the wet marble floor, through the steamy air into the whirlpool. Back straight, chin lifted, I stepped down into the bubbling water with what I hoped was the same steady grace as my sponsor.

Andrea motioned to me from across the circular hot tub, an invitation to join her on a narrow, underwater bench that was directly across from the ladies' semi-circle and the entire ten-foot length of the tub away. In slow motion, I moved toward her, finding the water gelatinous, resilient, buoyant. Inwardly, I shivered from heat.

At the bench I stopped before Andy's green eyes, before her glossy lips and flushed cheeks. Her blond eyelashes were darkened with damp; the hollow of her throat was slick. Less than half the bench lay empty beside her. There was no way to sit without sliding into her silken flesh, without causing our dripping shoulders to meet like lips in a chaste, tongue-less kiss. Then, on that underwater bench I felt our bare thighs connect—my right and her left. Andrea's skin was supple as water; for an instant I doubted the touch.

Not daring to look at Andy's face, I stared straight forward into a blurry middle distance, the semi circle of ladies in my peripheral vision. My right thigh felt the merest increase in pressure, so slight I couldn't be sure it had happened, couldn't be sure it was Andrea's intention instead of some motion of the bubbling water. I sat perfectly still, hardly daring to breathe, as below the water Andy's calf grazed mine. Her toned leg felt yielding, not hard like a man's. Her moon-round face was composed, her eyes shut, her damp lashes resting on heat-reddened cheeks.

Following Andrea's lead, I leaned my head back. My long, loose hair streamed into the water, feathered my breasts and shoulders as my eyes closed and my thighs slipped apart on the bench.

"Mmm," I heard Andy's throaty murmur as my flesh settled into hers.

"Andy?" I whispered.

"Hush." Her voice was low and light. Her hand moved underwater to my knee. "Hush," she repeated, as though comforting a child.

I felt unable to move or speak while between my legs, between the shorn lips of my bare vulva, there was a quiver. Then came the rise and stir of that narrow strip, blood rushing to the area, engorging the hidden sliver until it protruded from between my lower lips, lips swelling to open of their own accord, as yet untouched, caressed only by water. Then, while I pulsed with anticipation, Andy's hand began its slow journey up the inside of my thigh.

Across the tub, one woman spoke in a loud voice, "Bunny, what did you think of that new manicurist?"

"Not much," another answered. "Better keep your hands above the water though."

"Hot water peels the polish right off," the third agreed as Andrea's finger reached my slit.

Tears welled in my eyes as she traced those swollen lips. Tears of gratitude, tears of longing and sheer lust gathered as her finger gently skimmed, over and over, the surface of my throbbing sex. Then, at last she spoke in a whisper. "Lara, open your eyes."

I blinked into the harsh reality of the Hamilton Club, the semi-circle of female faces, the jade green marble floors, and lime green tiled tub. My eyes shut again, fast.

"Open your eyes, Lara." Her voice was insistent; her finger stroked my slit. Sometimes she grazed my throbbing *nub, others she skimmed just left or right. But when I didn't obey, her hand stopped cold. "Open," was all she said.*

Then, reluctantly, I opened again to the ladies' whirlpool at the famous Hamilton Club.

"Look at me," she commanded as her finger returned to its magic.

I turned to her fixed green gaze, and our eyes locked. A rush of relief came—as if her intensity could hold and embrace me, insulate us from all others, even transmit a measure of her own confidence and animal grace. My eyes drank in Andy's face while my clit screamed out for her touch. No longer was her fingertip enough; I craved, begged, demanded more.

"Darling, you know they can't find decent service people here," complained a cultured voice from across the whirlpool. "The new elevator man is quite impertinent."

Andrea's finger stroked with infinite patience, with infinite lightness of touch. She made circles, grazing the most tender, swollen part of my clit. "I want you to do something for me." She spoke in a low voice.

I was barely able to nod.

"It's a hard thing, but it's going to make you stronger." Her finger flicked my clit. "Will you do it?" Another flick. "Will you trust me?"

"Yes." It was more a breath than a word.

"But you must admit the masseuse they hired last month is pretty good," came a voice from across the tub.

"If you like that sort of pressure," was her friend's reply.

"Turn your face toward those women," Andy whispered, indicating them with her chin.

"C-can't." I stuttered.

Her finger shot into me, penetrated my opening for the first time. "Bad girl."

"Oh, God." Tears came to my eyes; her forefinger slid in and out.

"Do what I say and you'll get strong." Her thumb covered my clit.

Teardrops leaked out, ran down my cheeks. My lips mouthed the word, "Please."

"Listen to me, Lara. It doesn't matter what those women think."

I stifled a sob as her expert fingers played my private parts.

"You try too hard," Andrea continued. "Some people love that. Bosses love it." Her tone was emphatic; her fingers never stopped. "But you're too old for that now. Grow up, Lara. Take life on your own terms; honor your needs and desires, instead of worrying what others think."

"I know, I know," I murmured as the tears trickled down my face.

"You can do this." Her voice was fire. Her finger moved in and out. "Now."

My head turned; my brown eyes released the shelter, the anchor of her green ones. Andy's hand kept caressing my sex while my face turned toward the semi-circle of ladies. As if that trio knew something was happening, as if they sensed some subtle energy shift, the group grew quiet; their eyes focused on me.

"That's good." Andy's voice at my ear became a lifeline. She penetrated me with a second finger. "See the woman on the far left?"

I shot a quick glance at the snub-nosed, forty-something brunette.

"I want you to make eye contact with her."

My eyes lowered.

"No," she hissed, fingers plunging. "You can do this."

"Andy," I pleaded.

"No!" Her jaw clamped; her fingers stabbed. "Don't do it for me," she said between gritted teeth. "Do it for yourself."

I felt the bright eyes of the snub-nosed lady burning on my face. But somehow I forced my own gaze to meet them. My lips trembled, but my eyes held steady. A moment later, my heart swelled.

"Yes, my lovely, yes, my sweet," Andrea crooned beside me, stroking my clit and rhythmically thrusting her fingers.

Tears coursed down my cheeks again; they flowed freely, cleansing my face as I presented it to that semi-circle of strangers. I didn't care that the snub-nosed woman saw me crying. I didn't care if the whole semi-circle stared. At that moment, nothing mattered more than my connection to Andy and the sensations searing my body.

"Can I help you?" the snub nosed woman asked in a shrill voice. Somehow I managed to shake my head without looking away.

"Good work," Andrea said after a long moment. "Go to the next one. Let her see you too."

The second woman was pixie-like and freckled, with short, curly hair. But her eyes were narrowed with disapproval, and her mouth pursed like a prune. I felt her grim stare tear my chest apart, rip my ribcage open, left and right, like a pair of French doors. Yet, as Andy's fingers continued to thrust, as the tears slipped down my cheeks, I found I could take it. I could let her see me. Even when she asked with false brightness, "Is something wrong, dear?" I merely shook my head no, reveling in the certainty that— while raw emotions were visible on my face—beneath the water all was private.

Yes, that pixie-faced woman saw everything and nothing; she could make of it what she would. But I was free to meet her stare; her opinion no longer controlled me. Exulting in the weird, heady freedom of exposure, I felt Andrea beam at me, still thrusting.

"Now the last one," she said.

I turned my attention to the final woman, my body trembling with terror and joy. She was the oldest, her hair silvering at the temples, wrinkles creasing her forehead. Smiling, she nodded.

Somehow I managed to return that nod while A's fingers pierced me. Then I heard A's voice say loud and strong, "Lara Leeds, I'd like you to meet Bunny Harper, Claire Sanford, and Mary Barton."

They nodded politely as I forced a raw, but triumphant "hello."

If only those women had gotten out of the tub and left me alone with Andy's fingers! But I was condemned to their company as wave after wave of torturous pleasure washed over me, bringing me ever closer to a climax that I couldn't reach in their presence. Finally Andrea's fingers pulled out, and in a tender gesture, her hand cupped my pulsing sex.

Leaning close to my ear, her lips brushing the lobe, she whispered, "Sauna," and rose from our underwater bench. Then she walked to the steps of the hot tub, giving the trio of ladies a quick wave.

I followed fast, no longer giving a thought to my nakedness as I rose, dripping, from the whirlpool. Like Andy, I grabbed a towel from the pile waiting on a shelf and wrapped it around my waist. Then, I followed her to the dimly lit, cedar-scented sauna. Finally, we were alone. Andrea spread her towel on one wooden shelf-bench, and I took another.

"I hope you don't mind," she said, lying down on her back, "but I made us both manicure appointments."

"Manicure?" I repeated stupidly, as my entire trembling, tingling skin cried out for A's touch.

"Seven o'clock appointment." Her tone was matter-of-fact. "That gives us ten minutes."

So one of us still knew what time it was, and cared. One of us still had a schedule. And incredibly, we stayed on that schedule; nothing else unusual happened. We had our manicures, followed by herbal tea. A didn't invite me to her room or touch me again until it was time to say good-bye. Then, in a quiet corner of the ladies' dressing room, when both of us were fully clothed, Andy reached out and pulled me toward her. Clasping her long arms around my back—we were the only ones present—pressing her chest against mine, she stage-whispered, "A+ on your hot tub lesson."

Then her mouth brushed mine; her tongue parted my lips, darting inside to command and explore. After a long moment, she broke away, laughing, and slapped my butt, hard.

I flinched at the slap and the sudden change. My ass cheek stung, but it was nothing compared with my stinging clit, which was—once again—electrified.

Then Andrea called a car service and arranged for a driver to take me home, no easy feat in a NYC thunderstorm. Later, alone, in my own bedroom, I pulled out the gift her husband had sent me from Asia: the Ben Wa balls. I lubricated and inserted them, pressed my largest vibrator—turned on high—to my clit and dreamed of my beautiful, blond Valhalla Viking while the weighted metal balls her husband sent from Tokyo vibrated deep inside me.

Gala Cocktail Benefit

Commemorating

The Memorial Sloan-Kettering

Pediatric Oncology center
June 20, 2013

5:00PM – 8:00PM

The Water Club
23rd Street and
the East River

Admit One

From the Desk of Andrea Thane
Final Draft for Intro Speech 6/20

Robbie. Rob. Bob. Bobby. These were the names my husband, Sam, and I once thought we'd be calling our son. Robert Samuel Thane would have been twelve this year. His father and I chose that name carefully, thinking it would have to last our son a lifetime.

We imagined we'd only get away with "Robbie" when he was little. Then we'd move to "Rob"—or maybe "Bob" if he was a sporty type. "Bobby" could come later, when he got old enough to charm the girls, and "Robert" was sufficiently formal for an adult, no matter what line of work he chose.

But Sam and I never got past Robbie. Our little towheaded boy was five years old when he died from Leukemia, despite bone marrow transfusions, seven long years ago. Our son never stopped being Robbie, and he never will. Robbie never graduated from kindergarten or learned how to read, but he did get the kindest, most compassionate, and up-to-date medical care available at that time.

Sloan-Kettering was there for our son seven years ago, and today, thanks to the generosity of people like you, the Pediatric Oncology Center at The Memorial Sloan-Kettering is offering even better in-patient and out-patient care. More than ever, today we treat the whole child—including his or her family and even close friends in the process whenever possible.

Our Pediatric Pavilion is family-centered, using lots of natural light, color, art, and technology. Our Day Hospital is equipped with crafts, video games, baking, and a special area for toddlers. Not only medical care, but also a life affirmative atmosphere is necessary for healing. A hospital can no longer be a mere factory hoping to cure desperately ill children. For some kids, like my son, Robbie, the hospital is the milieu in which a great deal of time is spent. Now, time is precious to all of us, but for some children it is also sadly scarce.

That's one reason why not only medical treatments, but also the supporting staff, emotional care, and environment of a hospital are so important. On behalf of Memorial Sloan-Kettering and as the mother of five-year-old Robbie Thane, I would like to thank you for your heartfelt generosity up to now and also to entreat you to continue giving liberally to a cause that's so obviously noble in a world full of ambiguities.

Please take a moment to fill out the cards on your tables before leaving. And thank you very much.

It is now my great honor to introduce our keynote speaker, the brilliant Dr. Frederick Tanner, a forerunner in bone marrow research, who, we are proud to say, recently joined our team at Sloan-Kettering.

**To Benefit the Pediatric Cancer Center
Memorial Sloan-Kettering**

Please consider making a donation today.
Contributions are tax deductible.

All gifts are appreciated and no donation is too small

Friend $1-$99 **Supporter** $100-$249 **Sponsor** $250-$999
Angel $1,000-$4,999 **Patron** $5,000-$9,999
Benefactor $10,000-$99,999
Pacesetter $100,000 and above

Check enclosed or charge my credit card
_____-_____-_____ exp. date: __/__/__

Name as it appears on the card_____

Address_____

Signature_____

If your corporation has a matching funds policy, check here __
If you'd like to receive information on how to set up a trust or
leave Sloan-Kettering a bequest in your will, check here__

**Interested in volunteering personal time or other resources?
Contact Andrea Thane at (212) 555-3536 or
*AndreaThane@gmail.com***

Andrea Thane is organizing volunteers for a wide variety of
services and events, from fundraising to working directly with
children. Please feel free to call her with your questions and
suggestions. Remember, your continued commitment is our most
valuable resource.

Subject: nervous and confused
Date: 6/20/2013   11:23 PM
From: *LLeeds@ThanePR.com*
To: *HAltman@AltmanGizmo.com*

Henry, you're either psychic or a very gifted bloodhound
with power to sniff out the facts over the airwaves of the
internet. Yes, mea culpa, you're right; something did
happen at the Hamilton Club. What tipped you off? I barely
mentioned the whirlpool and sauna. The truth is I don't feel
comfortable telling you the whole story. I mean, I haven't
told anyone. (The only place I feel right about expressing
what happened is my journal—now *there's* a racy book.)
Honestly, my relationship with Andy is more than a little
embarrassing. Plus, I notice you're not sending me a
detailed description of your sex life.

Speaking of which, Henry, what's going on for you? You
haven't mentioned a girlfriend, but when I think of you in a
group house, I must admit my imagination runs wild. Have
you tried to recreate our thing with Terry? Or is that why
you're sweet-talking me—offering to find me a lift to the
ferry and let me sleep in the best room in your house?

Well, old buddy, old pal, that invitation will have to wait a
tad longer because I AM GOING CRAZY. It's all my own
fault, but what *are* the protocols for girl-on-girl action? Does
the rule about calling the next day apply to same sex
situations? Shit, shit! I feel like an absolute idiot. Sitting by
the phone, waiting for a *woman* to call. And, in the
meantime, my hot lover—HER HUSBAND/MY BOSS—just
got back from his business trip. He'll be in the office
tomorrow, and God knows what he'll want. . . .

I hate to say it, but I'm kind of dreading seeing Sam. I
confess, at the best of times he's a little scary, but now . . .

NERVOUS! I mean, having a thing with the boss's wife, WHAT WAS I THINKING? I could lose my job in the blink of an eye. Or—do you think I could sue for sexual harassment? (Only kidding, ha, ha.)

The worst part is: while Andy's not calling me, she's probably with *him*. They're probably together, having a romantic dinner somewhere expensive, like adults who left their pesky kid at home. I bet Sam took her someplace fancy, someplace he'd never take me. I wonder how he treats her in bed? I wonder how *she* treats *him*. Oh God, Henry, this is worse than sitting next to the wall, listening to you and Terry fuck. And that was pretty bad.

Henry, Henry, you better not be shocked, because I think it's time to horse trade. You've got to email back and tell me something about your relationships or else I will die of embarrassment. I'm depending on your sense of fairness, old buddy. Let's hear some juicy goings on from your Fire Island abode. You want me to visit sooner than mid-July? You're dying for a glimpse of me in my bikini? All right, then intrigue me, entice me, lure me out.

I'll be on the lookout for that sexy email,
Lara

Lara Leeds | Administrative Assistant
THANE PR INC.
117 Times Square, 3rd Floor, New York, NY 10036
☎direct phone (212) 555-0843
www.ThanePR.com

Subject: Fund Raiser
Date: 6/21/2013   12:05 PM
From: *BBlain@ThanePR.com*
To: *AndreaThane@gmail.com*

Dear Andrea,

This kind of letter should be written in longhand, so please forgive my email. I have all the modern excuses—being rushed etc.—but I feel ashamed to use them.

Andrea, it's been years since we were close, but last night with you and Sam felt like old times. I hope you won't mind my saying, while your dedication to Sloan-Kettering is impressive, I worry about what it costs you.

Yesterday, I recognized the stiff, startled look that still claims your face whenever you talk about Robbie. But I felt quite privileged when you sat down after speaking and let me fuss over you a bit. Lately it's hard to recall a time when you liked my taking care of you.

Remember after Robbie was first born and I got to play grandma? No, let's call that "aunt." Oh Andrea, I won't point out, one more time, how much you've changed. You know, I still have that little red plastic airplane, remember? Robbie forgot it at my apartment the last time he played there.

I miss the days when we were friends, Andrea. I miss the person you used to be almost as much as I miss Robbie. Is that a terrible thing to say? I miss the way Sam was in the old days too. You were such a great couple before.

Andrea, please don't be angry if I've overstepped my bounds. I really just meant to say thanks for including me.

It was a lovely evening,

Beth

Beth Blain | Office Manager
THANE PR INC.
117 Times Square, 3rd Floor, New York, NY 10036
☎direct phone (212) 555-0845
www.ThanePR.com

Subject: re: horse trading
Date: 6/21/2013   11:25 PM
From: *LLeeds@ThanePR.com*
To: *HAltman@AltmanGizmo.com*

Henry, you're an absolute prince, and your horse-trading isn't bad either. I'd go so far as to say you've got a real flair for barter, although I'm not quite ready to show you my journal—no matter how well written you think it must be. Seriously though, I want to thank you for setting me at ease. You always did have a generous nature, even shared your girlfriend with me once upon a time. Of course, Terry and I didn't exactly leave you unattended.

Anyway, I'm happy to hear that your exploits continue. Your moonlight swim with Kelly sounds like something out of a romantic movie—except for the part about freezing water and sticky grains of sand. I always wondered what happened to people who made it on the beach—all those gritty little grains of sand. I figured some of it got stuck in delicate places, even if you were careful and laid a blanket down.

You gave me a chuckle, Henry, and that's not an easy thing to do right now. Thinking of you naked on a damp towel, under the stars with a beautiful girl, trying to brush the sand off your erection till it was smooth enough to enter her—what an image! Of course, couldn't Kelly have cleaned you with her tongue? Unless she was afraid to get sand in her mouth, it does seem the obvious way. However, I don't want to cast aspersions on your current partner, whatever her reasons for not licking you clean. I'm sure she's just lovely, and not everyone likes oral sex as much as I do! Incidentally, does Kelly play the guitar? (Only kidding!)

Well, Henry, as you pointed out in your email, you're now entitled to another installment in my drama. So here's an episode synopsis: deranged young woman has sex with dark-haired boss while conjuring images of his blond wife. Yes, the first moment Sam kissed me with his dark-red lips, I flashed on Andy's coral ones and recalled the single time her mouth met mine.

When Sam Thane ran his tongue under the arch of my foot, up my ankle and calf, into the crease behind my knee— while I lay on my back on his possum fur bedcover, watching the top of his close-cropped, curly head approach the moist spot between my legs—instead of reveling in the sweet wet tease, I kept wondering if he'd licked his wife the night before. I kept thinking about Sam's tongue caressing Andy's feet, calves, thighs, and the sturdy, coiffed blond tulip between them. How did she taste, compared to me? My mind wouldn't stop.

In that state, I couldn't trust my perceptions, but Sam seemed off too. Before last night, he'd always been so *present*. His intensity, whether tender or gruff, had impacted me like a Zen master's slap. Yes, Sam was expert at shocking me into the moment, into an on-going, all-consuming experience that blotted out extraneous thought. In the past his caresses had ignited my chest with longing while his commands had stung my flesh. His fierce desire had awakened a twin flame inside me, and I'd been on fire when we were together, every word and gesture charged with risk and promise.

Henry, you know what I'm talking about. As you said in your email, "three years ago we all came alive in a profound way." I saw it in your face at the time. Like being at the still point in the center of a storm, silence becomes active, filling your brain, absorbing the usual chatter. Or there might be one word, like: *now* or *yes.* Or even: *no.* Just one word—throbbing the entire surface of your skin, pulsing through your muscles and deeper down into your hidden core. And that word is enough. All you need is NOW—reverberating through your being like an electrical charge. YES—unifying restless spirit and yearning flesh. NO—any more would be impossible.

But you *can* take more, and you *do* take more. The next time. Because you have to go farther to stay in the same place. And you feel thrilled and terrified moving past your comfort level, like looking down from the top of a black diamond slope until suddenly you realize you're already skiing—heading downhill with heartrending speed, traversing the mountain with undreamed delight. And something transcendent happens then; something essential and hidden becomes obvious and cherished. Your vulnerability turns into strength; you're purged of shame, and your needs feel potent, organic, embracing.

That's how sex can be at its best, the way it was when we were together—you and Terry and me. Henry, it feels kind of awkward putting all this in words, but I know you'll understand. Besides, you were so frank (and funny) about your beach experience—its limits and delights—that I hardly have the right to be embarrassed. God knows, I giggled out loud reading your email. And I've had my share of sticky sex situations; last night was one of them.

Honestly, Henry, it was chaos—thoughts whirling through my head while my body went nearly numb. Sam's blue eyes sparkled at me, but I couldn't stop worrying about the gaze he'd given Andy the night before—whether it had held more tenderness or respect. Then, when Sam's hands pressed my thighs apart, I couldn't help wondering if they'd spread his wife's legs wide twenty-four hours earlier. I imagined him lapping Andy's inner petals with his tongue, penetrating her hidden depth with his fingers, piercing and claiming her as he did me.

Andrea Thane was in the room, shimmering over the bed like a luminous shadow. Her gorgeous ghost haunted Sam and me, revealing the triangle we'd always been, but that I'd previously managed to ignore. Yes, Andy's apparition completed our de-facto *ménage a trois*, and for the first time, Sam's darting, swirling tongue couldn't bring me to orgasm.

Release only came when he finally took me the way a woman cannot. But even then, as my insides shuddered, the golden ghost plagued me. I couldn't stop thinking: how had my Nordic goddess received her husband from Tokyo this weekend? And was the fabulous Andrea Thane really reconciled to Sam's routine betrayal?

Henry, I know she'd never confront Sam about me; that scene would be way too undignified. And Andy has something to hide now, too. Oh God, it all makes me so NERVOUS. Before I met Andy, I felt superior—my being the "other woman," her being the cheated-on wife. But now I know Sam must love her—what man wouldn't? And a woman like Andy wouldn't stay with a man she didn't adore, especially an unfaithful one.

I'm probably just suffering a dose of reality; you can see the state I'm in. A fit of jealousy like the ones I used to have when I was little and my parents took their romantic weekend trysts. I hate this kind of stupid stuff that the school shrink made me talk about senior year. Being an only child, dangling from the tip of an isosceles triangle while my lovebird parents cooed to each other a long hypotenuse away.

Henry, Henry, I'm a disgrace. I should probably get a referral from that college shrink. Thank God I bumped into you at the Frick. Since my roommate moved out, there's been no one to talk to. No one I can trust, that is—until you. Yes, I'm grateful to the gods for bringing you back into my life. Henry, beam the healing force of your understanding out through cyberspace to your old friend. And thanks (again, in advance) for all your support.

Gratefully,
Lara

Lara Leeds | Administrative Assistant
THANE PR INC.
117 Times Square, 3rd Floor, New York, NY 10036
☎direct phone (212) 555-0843
www.ThanePR.com

Subject: re your impossible suggestions
Date: 6/22/2013   11:45 PM
From: LLeeds@ThanePR.com
To: HAltman@AltmanGizmo.com

Henry,

Thanks for the compliment on my writing. You really think I
could earn extra bucks penning porn? Wow! And you
haven't even seen my journal. And your other idea is even
crazier—calling Andy or writing her a note—I'd rather die.

More bad news, they're raising my rent. You know, my
roommate got married and moved out of town six months
ago; I think I mentioned that. It's been awful having no one
to confide in; I'm so glad we reconnected.

Anyway, I've been trying to swing the apartment alone, but
it's TCFC. (Too close for comfort.) Have I told you anything
about my place? Other than noise from trucks going over
pot holes on Second Avenue, it's actually kind of great.

I've got a corner one bedroom with lots of light. Plus the
kitchen appliances were almost new when my roommate
signed her lease (two years ago).

Where do you live these days, when it isn't summer? Back
in Ann Arbor, you were the one—out of all of us—that had
your heart set on New York City. Did you ever find that
funky Greenwich Village apartment you'd planned out in
your head? If so, I'd love to see it. Do you live alone in the
winter?

I hate to admit how much I miss my roommate, but it's
awful watching videos by myself. Whatever. This is my

worst email yet. I almost deleted the whole thing. I'm hitting the send button before I change my mind.

Forgive the whining,

Lara

Lara Leeds | Administrative Assistant
THANE PR INC.
117 Times Square, 3rd Floor, New York, NY 10036
☎direct phone (212) 555-0843
www.ThanePR.com

Subject: Mock-ups
Date: 6/23/2013   10:15 AM
From: *SThane@ThanePR.com*
To: *BBlain@ThanePR.com*

Beth,

Thanks for dropping off those mock-ups at the Hamilton;
you saved me a trip to the office. I'm jazzed about the look
our creative team came up with for the Back-to-School
promo. My gut still says that demographic is big for
Makashi—despite the stubborn old goat's refusal to see it. If
the samples you dropped off don't convince him, nothing
will.

Unfortunately, as the days drag by, we lose precious time.
It's going to be too late for a back-to-school campaign if the
fool hesitates any longer. Makashi has got to hit North
America first. I want Thane PR to make Makashi a cool
status symbol for teens—in a variety of eye catching colors.

Beth, Andy and I enjoyed having you at the fund raiser, but
things have changed since the old days. No one knows that
better than you. I need you to respect the relationship Andy
and I have evolved over the last few years —as you, of all
people, know—not without considerable pain.

Which reminds me, Beth, Andy is not mad at you. As I said
yesterday on the phone, she's not the least bit offended by
your email. So stop worrying, OK? And try to leave Lara
Leeds alone. I know you think you're being loyal to Andy,
and I appreciate that. But, as you and I have discussed many

times, my wife is a big girl, more than capable of speaking on her own behalf.

Try taking life with a grain of salt, Beth. It's the only way to survive the heartache. Enough said. I take off for Tokyo tonight and will contact you from there with further updates.

Sam

Samuel H. Thane | President
THANE PR INC.
117 Times Square, 3rd Floor, New York, NY 10036
☎direct phone (212) 555-0842
www.ThanePR.com

LARA

June 23, 2013

Dear Andy,

    I know you're probably busy, but I thought I'd just drop a quick note into the mail. (I'm hoping they'll forward this if you're no longer at the Hamilton Club.) Anyway, Andy, thank you so much for the manicure and spa date. I really appreciate all you've done for me.

    Sorry if this letter seems a bit late; I just haven't had a free moment these last few days. However, I wanted you to know how much I enjoyed our time together.

Warmly,
Lara

Subject: I did it
Date: 6/23/2013   11:32 PM
From: *LLeeds@ThanePR.com*
To: *HAltman@AltmanGizmo.com*

Well, I hope you're proud of me: I sent Andy a note. Guess I'm not the coward I thought I was. Especially with a little encouragement from you. Really, Henry, thanks for helping me get up the guts. Not that I've stopped torturing myself, of course. Now I ruminate about her return emails. Yada, yada, yada, it never stops. Meantime, Sam's coming for a last visit; he probably told Andy he was heading for the airport. How much do you want to bet he shows up with a suitcase?

Listen Henry, I'm still not quite ready to let you read my journal, even if you're right about my hiding all my best writing there. Tell you what, in a thousand years when I become the pornographer of your dreams, we'll read portions of it aloud to each other, OK? And speaking of sex—our favorite topic—what kind of kinky stuff are you and Kelly into? Any more midnight swims? Maybe she'll invite you to live with her after the summer ends, or isn't it that kind of relationship? If you'd like, I could see what's available in this building. It's weird you lived in Greenwich Village two years and I never knew. Too bad about losing your rent controlled walk-up; you'll never find anything else in Manhattan for that price. Uh oh, the buzzer—gotta go.

Lotsa luv, Lara

Lara Leeds | Administrative Assistant
THANE PR INC.
117 Times Square, 3rd Floor, New York, NY 10036
☎direct phone (212) 555-0843
www.ThanePR.com

Subject: checking in
Date: 6/24/2013   6:15 PM
From: *AndreaThane@gmail.com*
To: *SThane@ThanePR.com*

Sam dear,

What am I going to do with you? Flying all the way from Tokyo to New York just to watch me deliver a speech that's similar to hundreds you've heard before. What a sweet, stupid thing to do! Sometimes I think you're the loyalist dog around while others, well . . .

Who else could evoke such conflicting feelings? Saturday night you were exasperating, making good your promise to drive me crazy as only you know how. Your lips, tongue, hands—no one teases like you, Sam. No one makes me cry out and beg for more, until I come—over and over— in ripples and waves, like I'm going for the world's record.

Darling, you seemed so *present* on Saturday; you made me feel present too. Even at the gala, something felt different. It couldn't have been because Beth was there? Maybe enough time has finally passed for us to look each other in the eye again. It's been years since I felt your gaze linger on me, years since our eyes met during sex, since you pierced me with your stare and your cock at the same time. No, we haven't been together like that in almost a decade.

Time hasn't aged your body much, Sam. You still have the physique—and stamina—of the athlete you were when we first met. Giving the devil his due, I have to admit: your workout fanaticism has paid off for both of us. Thanks for getting me started, my dear, sixteen long years ago. Now—when, by rights, both our bodies should be approaching middle age—we're still fit to frolic with the lights on. My eyes (and hands and mouth) still savor your muscular legs, lean torso and solid, yet eminently squeezable, buttocks.

Yes, you're quite the stud, my love—as evidenced by our broken condom. That's something new, a first for us, after all these years. Good thing I'm forty-one and really past the age of worrying. Nevertheless, no more Trojans; next time we'll use a different brand. Still, I must admit, there's nothing quite like having you inside me au natural. Too bad we didn't ride bareback since that condom proved useless anyway.

Well, how effusive of me—that's quite enough complimenting for you. I must find something to scold you about soon. However, I'm obligated to impart a little good news first: our apartment is nearly habitable. The contractor says the cabinets are almost finished; with no further delays, I'll be home by the end of this week. Here's hoping your project winds up with as much speed as mine. And God bless Makashi's new clothing line for teens.

Love, Andy

Subject: lunch tomorrow
Date: 6/25/2013   10:05 AM
From: *AndreaThane@gmail.com*
To: *BBlain@ThanePR.com*

Beth dear,

I don't like to think of you worrying about me or yearning for the old days. I hadn't realized you felt so cast aside. Please forgive my selfishness. A certain odd numbing—of both experience and perception—is my only explanation for the evident blindness that has allowed me to be so insensitive to Robbie's de-facto aunt.

Although I have no sisters, I can't imagine that a blood sibling could have been any more generous or attentive at the crucial moments than you were. If my own mother were still alive, she couldn't have tended to Robbie and me with more loving care.

I've been remiss on a debt of gratitude, and I'd like to apologize. Perhaps lunch tomorrow would offer some compensation? Can I pick you up at the office at one o'clock?

Warmest regards,

Andrea

Subject: Can I come out this weekend?
Date: 6/24/2013   1:15 PM
From: *LLeeds@ThanePR.com*
To: *HAltman@AltmanGizmo.com*

Oh God, Henry, just take me out and shoot me!

Not only did the Nordic Ice Goddess <u>not</u> send an email reply to my note, but she stopped by the office a few minutes ago and took my arch enemy Beth Blain, the office manager, out to lunch.

I checked at the reception desk, to see if Andy might have left me a discreet note. But no. Nothing. Nil. Zip. Nada. And the elegant Mrs. Andrea Thane—head held high on her long white neck—didn't so much as blink a blond eyelash or raise a tweezed brow as she sailed past my desk. I feel like such an idiot.

Henry, you don't think that could have been Andy's plan all along? To make me feel stupid and ashamed? Honestly, I'm beginning to wonder . . .

I'd like to accept your standing invitation and flee to Fire Island this weekend. If you feel so inclined, you can ply me with liquor while I moan about the pitfalls and politics of office sex. Or we can take long walks on the beach together, slathering sun tan lotion on each other during the day and looking for constellations in the sky at night.

Or, if you prefer, I could be boring and promise not to make Kelly jealous. I could offer her a lesson in the fine art of emergency sand removal techniques. Only teasing. But I'm deadly serious about coming out this weekend.

Henry, my friend, could you possibly receive an emergency guest this Friday? I know it's short notice, but I've got to get out of here!

Hoping for safe harbor,

Lara

Lara Leeds | Administrative Assistant
THANE PR INC.
117 Times Square, 3rd Floor, New York, NY 10036
☎direct phone (212) 555-0843
www.ThanePR.com

Journal—June 24, 2013

*At the liquor store Andrea wore an elegant white
linen suit and silk camisole. A triple strand of pearls was
tight at her throat; above it, a wide-brimmed, white hat and
sunglasses made her seem taller than ever. But when
Andy's emerald eyes peered up over her dark lenses,
thoughts of the office ceased.*

*Andrea selected a bottle of Patron Silver Tequila,
and I stood beside her at the checkout counter in my
summer slacks. Stunned by the sudden nearness of her
height and breadth—the sheer white and blond solidity of
her—I steadied myself by putting a hand on the countertop.
Andrea's hand went down too; her pinky grazed mine, and
sparks skimmed my wrist as the cashier rung up our
purchase. Then Andy's hot palm landed—burning—
between my shoulder blades; she propelled me out the
door.*

*On the sidewalk, she hailed a cab and gave the
Hamilton Club address. Neither of us spoke as the taxi flew
up Third Avenue and across 63rd Street to the vaunted Park
Avenue brownstone. Moments later Andrea unlocked her
door, revealing a Victorian-style bedroom: chintz chairs,
flowered fabrics, and a canopied, four-poster bed.*

"Sit down," she finally spoke.

*I obeyed while she removed her hat and twisted the
Tequila bottle open. Two glasses waited on the spindly-
legged, antique desk; Andy poured a splash in each.
"Drink." She handed one to me and watched while I took a
cautious sip. "The whole thing."*

*I tossed it back, pretending I'd done many shots of
tequila before. But when the liquor hit the back of my
throat, I couldn't help coughing.*

"Refill," she commanded, holding out the bottle.

Throat still burning, I extended my empty glass.

"Take your shirt off." Andrea poured the second shot and threw back her tequila as I gingerly sipped at mine. "Bra too."

I set my glass on the floor, and fingers shaking, undid the buttons of my blouse. As soon as my bra was visible, it embarrassed me with its plain, stretchy beige nylon that allowed my dark aureoles and nipples to show through.

"Off." She gave the offensive garment a toss of her golden head.

I was glad to get rid of it.

"Drink." She lifted my glass from the floor and brought it to my lips.

Naked from the waist up, I watched her gold-ringed, French-manicured hand tilt the cup to my mouth. Swallowing, I wondered how long it had been since a woman pressed a cup to my lips. Fifteen years, twenty? Then Andrea took an ice cube from the bucket on her antique table, knelt down before me in her white linen suit, and pressed the cube to one startled breast.

Cold shocked my nipple; I let out a tiny cry. A rivulet of water trickled down my chest, and Andy's hot mouth encircled one aureole. Her tongue was luxuriant, warm and wet; her teeth exerted light pressure. The hand with the ice cube moved to the small of my back; melting ice dripped down into my low waisted slacks, cooling the crack of my buttocks. On her knees before me, her long blond hair flowing around her broad shoulders, Andrea sucked and nibbled, teeth sinking deeper by degrees into my nipple. Her emerald eyes didn't close, but peered up at my face as she bit down hard.

"Bite," I heard my own voice beg.

She bit again in a slightly different spot—very hard, almost too hard— using her tongue at the same time. Then she released my breast to stand, stepping out of her pumps, removing her linen jacket. There was Andy's deep, shadowed cleavage, edged by the silk camisole's lacy décolletage. Around her long neck the triple-strand of pearls looked like an elegant collar.

"Lie back." She retrieved her empty glass from the floor and poured another tequila. "Unzip your pants."

I lay back on the flowered bedspread, beneath the Hamilton Club canopy while Andrea sipped her fresh tequila, leaving faint coral imprints on the glass. Her eyes seemed hard and haughty; the curve of her lips looked akin to a sneer.

"Take your pants off." Her tone had sharpened to match her face. "Leave your panties on."

My hands went clumsy with reluctance and shook unzipping my fly. Then, skin prickling with desire and dread, I lifted my hips and wriggled out of my slacks. Nearly naked on the four poster bed, I looked up at Andy as I'd watched her husband in the past: awaiting instructions, guessing and worrying about what might come next.

Head held high on her long white neck, Andrea's green eyes scanned my body. I couldn't help hating the skimpy, red satin-polyester panties I still wore, bought on sale at Victoria's Secret. In a flash I saw that lingerie through Andy's eyes—heartbreakingly vulgar, endlessly cheap. Her panties would match her silk camisole, I thought; they'd be imported from France, never purchased two for one from a sale bin. Inwardly cringing, I felt as cheap and ordinary as my polyester underwear, as naïve and ridiculous as a schoolgirl with my navy blue knee socks still on my feet.

Surprisingly, Andy seemed to like the socks. She approached my feet, rolled one down, and peeled it off with hands that were slow, tender, almost maternal. With the flat of her palm she caressed the sole of my foot. Then she smiled at me, a beautiful, full-lipped smile. "Masturbate," she said.

"What?" I managed, playing for time.

She let out a short laugh. "You heard me."

"But—" I stared up from the canopied bed, making my face a plea.

Andrea's lush coral lips pressed together; her strong jaw thrust forward. Without words, her message came clear: I'd already masturbated to please her husband; now I could do it for her.

"The sock," I whined, feeling faintly ridiculous, lifting my navy foot.

"I like the sock," her voice was steel. "Leave it on."

Then I understood: if I wanted Andy's hands, lips, tongue, I'd have to prostrate myself before her. Not her forgiveness, but her passion was available to me—at a certain price.

"Slide your hand under your panties, Lara."

She wanted me to do it with one sock on, wearing the vulgar red panties. There was to be no dignity in my surrender, only exposure and lust. Yes, lust still surged through my nearly naked body as I stared at Andy's face and recognized a tiny blemish on her skin—the kind I get when feeling hormonal. Below it, the thick pearl choker looked too tight for comfort.

"Do it, Lala." Her emerald eyes shone hard as glass, and I saw how my subjugation could be Andrea's victory, revenge against her husband and me.

"No," I whispered, but didn't move.

"Are you sure?" she asked after a moment, stepping back from the bed.

My eyes ran down to the hollow of her throat, scooped and delicate beneath her fancy necklace. How differently she acted from her husband, who'd never backed off, giving me room to choose. Andy's manicured hand rose to her throat; her fingers tugged at the pearls.

I swallowed, and my own throat constricted. But when I spoke my voice was strong, "Give me a minute."

Alert, expectant, and oddly patient, Andrea's green eyes rested on me. Her beautiful lips smirked, ironically, self referentially, as if responding to an inner voice. "Lara?"

So it was up to me. I could offer myself to the elegant and cultured Andrea Thane—or not. My bare and bitten nipples stirred; the crotch of my cheap panties grew wet. Andrea had been right when she said I underestimated myself. It was time to stop making that mistake.

"I'd like another tequila," I announced.

"Why not?" she agreed and poured.

Still sitting on the edge of the bed, I took a slow sip of Patron Silver Tequila and watched Andy's face above the glass. I became conscious of my lips pressing the smooth rim, soft and wet kissing cool and hard, tequila stinging my tongue. Then Andy's eyes moved over my face, down to my bare breasts, where my nipples were pointy with desire and reddened by her teeth. Her gaze made my shaven lower lips tingle; more moisture leaked onto my slinky red panties. Then Andrea's lips parted, and my clit perked as the pink tip of her tongue emerged to lick her upper lip.

That gesture, unlike so many of her others, seemed unpracticed and unplanned. It even seemed possible that Andy—who ordinarily exerted supreme self control—was unaware of how her straight white teeth had sunk into her lush lower lip. The expression touched me with its unexpected vulnerability. Could it be, I wondered, that Andrea's Achilles heel had been first camouflaged and now revealed by her need to contact and control me? I sucked my lower lip, wishing it was hers. Perhaps she'd written that original letter to gain the upper hand—first through intimidation and then seduction. Why didn't that make me mad?

Was it because I'd enjoyed the ride so much I didn't care what had fueled it? Dangling my legs off the edge of the bed, I swung my knee-socked calf back and forth, reflecting that even my education was to Andy's advantage. The stronger I became, the less suitable I'd be for her husband.

Andrea's green eyes narrowed on my swinging leg; her blond head tilted.

There, nearly nude on the edge of the bed, sipping tequila, I discovered that I enjoyed keeping her waiting. I enjoyed watching suspense and uncertainty play on her face, knowing I'd inspired those emotions. After finishing my third tequila, I rose to place my empty glass on the antique table. I knew better than to drink anymore.

On my way back to the bed, I made sure to move slowly, close to Andy's body, grazing her tapered skirt with my hip. Cheap red satin slithered audibly across classic white linen as I passed the round of my butt by her pelvis.

"What are you doing?" Andrea asked, surprised.

"Being naughty." I lay back down beneath the canopy, spread my legs and tented my knees. Using a pillow, I propped up my head to look straight at Andy's face. "Masturbating." The word felt mealy in my mouth. I've never liked to say it. "Masturbating," I made myself repeat, snaking my hand under my panties to where my clit was already wet.

A smile stretched across Andrea's face. She approached the bed and stood so close her knees touched the mattress. "Are you sure?" she asked with a hitch in her voice.

"I want to." My eyes stayed open to meet her gaze. Open to whatever they'd see in her luminescent features, open for whatever they'd reveal. Had the tequila emboldened and crazed me, or had I just come too far to turn back? For a week, I'd wanted and thought of nothing but Andy; now I had to have her. Now—in the quaint old fashioned Hamilton Club bedroom— this was our moment. I wouldn't get another chance.

Under the red panties, my forefinger stroked my slit. Then I spoke without speaking, let my eyes pose the question: Is this what you want? Me, one-socked and debased on the bed—you watching with linen and pearls?

Andrea's green eyes glistened; her coral lips curved in her moon round face.

I'm doing it willingly, I telegraphed to her. I give it to you as a gift. Not to compensate for being with Sam—we both know that's impossible. Not to gain your approval or affection—we're way past good impressions.

Knowing the truth, I let it shine through my face—while my fingertip grazed the length of my clit, back and forth, back and forth. I wanted this experience. I wanted Andy's fierce eyes, smooth hands, hot mouth—as much of herself as she'd be willing to share. I could go first, offering up my pride, suddenly needing to give my dignity away more than I needed to keep it. And as I let go, the word "paradox" filled my head along with an image of Henry Altman lying naked on his college bed, his brown eyes wide with fear and longing, smiling up at Terry and me.

Then came Andrea's voice—cool and controlled. "Tweak your nipple," she said.

I brought my free hand to the breast that was already tender. Eyes still wide, focused on Andy, I pinched the sore nipple and let my face show the sweet ache. My clit quivered, reaching up to my finger, but I kept my stroking light. Andrea's pale face, her long neck, her ivory bosom with its lace décolletage loomed above me, while every fiber in my being cried out for more. More of her skin, mouth, gaze. Her body closer, pressed against me, her hands where mine were. Eyes still open, I allowed that longing to shape my face.

Then something Andrea had said at Vincent's café came back to me. "Humility," her cultured voice had intoned that first time we met. "Humility is the key, Lara, not humiliation."

"Andy," I began.

But she said, "Hush," the way she had in the hot tub. Then, slowly, green eyes steady on my brown ones, Andrea reached around to unzip her skirt. It fell to the floor, and for a long moment, she stood barefoot before me, in her ivory lace panties, camisole, and pearls.

Beneath the red panties, I caressed my clit, keeping my eyes open. Andy pulled off her camisole, releasing her big, creamy breasts, with their large petal pink aureoles. I sucked my lower lip hard, mouth hungry for her skin. At last in a single, swift and graceful gesture, Andrea stripped off the sliver of silk lace that had hidden her Georgia O'Keefe masterpiece.

"Don't stop masturbating," she told me, standing naked. "Don't stop," she reminded again, climbing onto the bed.

I kept my finger moving as Andrea lay down beside me, an ivory skinned goddess with flowing flaxen hair. On the flowered bedspread we were inches apart; I felt the heat from her skin. Then Andy's pale face moved toward mine, and her eyes finally closed as our lips met. Her tongue was aggressive in my mouth; her breasts thrust against me. Her strong arm curved around my back, pulling me closer, holding me tight and kissing me hard.

Still masturbating, I kissed Andy back—voraciously. After a few moments, her hand slipped down beside mine, inside the vulgar red panties. Her fingers found my wet clit, and began making rhythmic circles. Only then did her mouth release my lips long enough to whisper, "Touch me."

Andrea's tulip clef was warm and wet, unexpectedly soft and welcoming. I began carefully with the lightest touch, with infinite restraint, with a fingertip no firmer than a breeze. Next to mine, her body quivered, and my free hand reached around to stroke her butt. Andy circled my clit and I grazed hers, feeling it harden and engorge under my touch. *Lying on our sides, chest to chest, eyes closed now, we kissed in a full body embrace.*

When Andrea's finger finally pierced me, I kissed her long neck that still wore pearls. I kissed her forehead and her eyelids. Then I pierced her too, heard her sharp intake of breath.

"Andy," I said. "Look at me."

Her green eyes flicked open and met mine. An instant later, a smile curved her lips. I smiled back, and we stared at each other beneath the canopy on the Hamilton's four poster bed. I watched Andrea and she watched me while our fingers stroked and thrust into each other. When I reached the point of orgasm, my eyes longed to shut. And for a while I thought release would be impossible if they didn't. Still stroking Andy, I teetered on the brink for an unbearable time; I don't know how long that lasted.

Andrea was struggling too; I saw it in her emerald eyes, in her cheeks stretched tight, in her full and twisted lips. I moved my hand over her buttocks, brought my forefinger to the crack. Then I traced that divide and slipped down between her cheeks to find the dark, tight, hidden hole. Andy's elegant face distorted; her body went rigid; her breathing stopped. She began to shake, and watching her, I shook too, as wave after intense wave permeated my whole body.

After that we lay side by side, exhausted, and both fell asleep. When I awakened, the digital clock on Andrea's night table showed 5:20 PM. Too late to go back to the office. I maneuvered off the bed without disturbing Andy, who was sleeping, naked, her long blond hair fanned out on the flowered bedspread. I almost laughed out loud when I realized I was still wearing my red panties and a single navy sock.

Subject: Lara Leeds
Date: 6/25/2013 9:12 AM
From: *BBlain@ThanePR.com*
To: *SThane@ThanePR.com*

Sam, I thought I'd seen everything, but no—Miss Lara Leeds disappeared from the office yesterday about 2 PM and never returned. If you hadn't asked me to keep an eye on her, I wouldn't interfere, but I thought you might like to know that she darted out the door just moments after Andrea—who was sweet enough to take me out for lunch—left the office.

Now Sam, I hope my reporting this does not seem like prying. I respect you and always want to be both loyal and discreet. But Ms. Leeds's sudden disappearance is really too much! I am trying to run a business here—in your absence. Apropos of that, I want you to know that you can count on me for any task, however unpleasant. If there's any way at all I can help, just say the word.

I'm here for you,
Beth

Beth Blain | Office Manager
THANE PR INC.
117 Times Square, 3rd Floor, New York, NY 10036
☎direct phone (212) 555-0845
www.ThanePR.com

Subject: call me ASAP, (212) 555-1786
Date: 6/25/2013   8:15 AM
From: *LLeeds@ThanePR.com*
To: *HAltman@AltmanGizmo.com*

Henry, I just tried your phone number, but there was a
weird mechanical voice on the recording. I guess it's your
answering machine, although I wasn't inspired to leave a
long message, being a bit uncertain. So here's the scoop:
I'd really love to come out <u>tomorrow</u>, if that's at all
convenient.

It's not like me to skip work, but I'm feeling a tad reckless,
ready to call Thane PR, say I'm deathly ill, and take the
next two days off. You see, I ran out of the office around
mid-afternoon today, without telling a soul. The office
manager's probably furious, cc-ing hate notes (in memo
form) to Sam and me. But this afternoon, when the glorious
Andrea Thane finally summoned me for an immediate,
intimate rendezvous, I obviously couldn't refuse. Or, maybe
I could have Henry, but—damn the consequences—I
wanted to go with her so I did.

There's something satisfying about that. Leaving the office
without explanation or apology, it was quite a thrill. Of
course, common sense is bound to return sooner or later,
and then I'll try to patch things up—if that's still possible.
But I just thought, if it worked for you, that I could play
hooky on Fire Island. Take the next couple of days off and
create a long weekend for myself. While I've got the
momentum, I mean. While I'm barreling forward, feeling so
free.

You see, Henry, something happened yesterday that I don't
quite understand. That I've never experienced before. I'll
put it this way: Andy and I finally consummated—as much

as two women can—and it was great, really fantastic. But we're finished now; I can feel it in my skin. I don't exactly understand it, but I know it's true. My obsession with the boss's wife is over, and—well, I think I want to break up with my boss too.

The thought occurs to me: what if that's what Andy wanted all along? But you know, it doesn't even matter. I learned something from her, although I can't sum it up in a sentence. And you helped me a lot too Henry, with all your support and encouragement. (Even though some of your compliments are such obvious bunk—like when you wax poetic about my beauty—but please don't stop!)

Henry, it occurs to me that I might lose my job. A definite possibility—after rushing out of the office, playing hooky, diddling the boss's wife, and now looking for a graceful way to break up with the boss himself! Chances are something's going to hit the fan. No, it doesn't look good for the good guys. (If I'm still one of the good guys?) But before I face my just desserts, I'd like to spend a few days with you.

Henry, can you call as soon as you read this email and let me know if it's okay?

Luv ya, Lara

Lara Leeds | Administrative Assistant
THANE PR INC.
117 Times Square, 3rd Floor, New York, NY 10036
☎**direct phone (212) 555-0843**
www.ThanePR.com

Subject: Lara Leeds
Date: 6/25/2013   9:15 AM
From: *SThane@ThanePR.com*
To: *BBlain@ThanePR.com*

Beth, slow down. Nice that Andy took you to lunch. Has she been coming by the office often?

Re Lara, there's probably some logical explanation. For example, she got sick—too nauseated or dizzy to talk. For now, I want you to give her the benefit of the doubt. Lara's been a good employee for the most part, although I admit there's been trouble lately.

Beth, please believe me when I say I can handle this—and any other issues that arise with Lara—on my own. I'm sure you understand. OK, Beth, what I want you to do is this: observe and report—that's all. Don't make me get strict with you. Enough said.

Next and more important—Mr. Makashi finally approved our presentation for his new line. We're showing it to his 2 brothers and the rest of the board of directors the beginning of next week. (Naturally, 1 guy's out of town and we're delayed till he gets back.) Probably means things will drag on till next weekend. Beth, after this contract is signed, we're going to have a hell of an office party.

Sam
Samuel H. Thane | President
THANE PR INC.
117 Times Square, 3rd Floor, New York, NY 10036
☎direct phone (212) 555-0842
www.ThanePR.com

Subject: checking in
Date: 6/25/2013   9:25 AM
From: *SThane@ThanePR.com*
To: *AndreaThane@gmail.com*

Darling Andy,

Have you been researching things to scold me about? Don't
laugh, but I saved your last email, sentimental soul that I
am. Of course, I noticed something special about last
Saturday night too. Let's not speculate on why. How about
we just keep going the way we always do? Forging forward,
blindly ignoring both good and bad—only kidding, my love.
Or half kidding, which amounts to the same thing.

I understand you took Beth out for lunch. Very nice. Picked
her up at the office too. Anything unusual occur there?
Doing field work for scolding fodder? Darling, I've learned
to be as suspicious of our good times as our bad. So I
wouldn't be surprised if a fight erupted to flatten the
feelings we generated last Saturday. In fact, I've been
hesitant to return your email or remark on our evening at all.
Call me superstitious, but these last years our passion has
always been followed by too much pain. Maybe that's just
the way of the world. Anyway darling, don't do anything
crazy. Don't do anything I wouldn't do. And remember how
much I love you, no matter what.

Forever, Sam.
Samuel H. Thane | President
THANE PR INC.
117 Times Square, 3rd Floor, New York, NY 10036
☎direct phone (212) 555-0842
www.ThanePR.com

H. A.

9 AM, 6/27/2013

Good Morning Sleeping Beauty,

Lara, I didn't want to wake you—not after we stayed up so late last night talking. Not when you look so peaceful, curled up on your bed, with your long dark hair fanned across your shoulders. You must admit, I kept my promise and gave you my most comfortable accommodations.

But the weather's perfect: sun shining, breeze blowing, taste of saltwater in the air. It's a poem out there, Lara. Just what you need to soothe your frazzled nerves. I'm right outside the back door, waiting for you with a chaise lounge.

There's coffee on the stove and bagels on the kitchen counter. Oh, and in case you still love OJ, I stashed some Tropicana (sorry, it was all they had at the convenience store) in the fridge. So take your time, but hurry up! It's not nearly as much fun on the beach without you.

Last one in the water's a rotten egg,
Henry

PS. I've got the towels and sunscreen for both of us.

PPS. Hurry!

Subject: thanks for the weekend
Date: 6/30/2013   10:15 PM
From: *LLeeds@ThanePR.com*
To: *HAltman@AltmanGizmo.com*

Henry, what can I say? *Danke schön*, *gracias*, *merci*, and
wow! Thanks so much for harboring me over the weekend.
I'd almost forgotten how healing fun can be. Perhaps, as
you said, I've been masquerading as a Manhattan
sophisticate too long. It's been ages since I laughed till my
cheeks hurt. (Maybe since our Ann Arbor days?)

But I'm glad we had one night alone before your weekend
gang came. I don't know why you're so good to me, Henry.
Listening while I work through my issues out loud—that's
got to be a bore. You were so patient and non-judgmental;
you know, if the gizmo business ever fails, you'd make a
great therapist. Here's a kooky snapshot for you: I become
a porno writer (yeah, yeah, I know you said "erotic writer")
and you become a shrink. Wouldn't that be hilarious? If,
after all my hard work at Thane PR, plus a closet of costly
(for me, anyway) corporate outfits, I ended up writing sex
stories for a living. And if, after all your years of tinkering
with gadgets, you ended up tinkering with people's minds,
using your natural clarity to parse out psyches instead of
small mechanics.

Yikes, how did I get started on all that? What I meant to do
was talk about the weekend. Your cottage is charming.
(Although I see why you can't stay there all winter. It'd be
way too cold and draughty, not to mention isolated after the
ferries go to their off season schedule.) But Henry, your
share people were so friendly—including me in all their
madcap games. Of course it helped that their fearless
leader (you) gave me a great introduction. But I loved
cocktails and kite flying, dirty jokes around the campfire.

You've got everything so organized, Henry; it reminds me of our Ann Arbor house, but without school work, like a summer camp for adults. And the campers look up to you too. When you collected funds for food and distributed the tasks involved in our barbecue, I was surprised to see six people pitch in so eagerly and without complaint. Did you whip your weekenders into shape at the beginning of the summer or hand pick them for their cooperative talents?

Anyway I really felt you've surrounded yourself with good people, and I was quite honored when they chose me to judge the weekly sand castle contest. But it wasn't easy watching you build a castle with Kelly. The green eyed devil flew onto my shoulder, and his sharp little claws dug into my back each time her suntan oil slick skin slid over yours. Yes, I had quite the collection of puncture marks by the time the weekend was over. Of course, I'm not really jealous. I haven't got the right. And God knows, there's enough on my plate right now.

But I do want to thank you for being sensitive to my feelings. Yes, I noticed the way you glanced at me when Kelly kissed you hello Friday night, the way you tried to inject a little distance whenever I was around. Kelly's lucky. I swear, I almost felt like Andrea Thane, watching you two together. It crossed my mind to try my prowess befriending your girlfriend and then scaring her off. (Only kidding, old buddy, I promise.) But I have to hand it to Andy; it *is* an interesting strategy. However, I'm off women lovers now, at least for a while.

So Henry, where was I? Oh yes, thanking you for the weekend—for the sun and the sea and the sand. The weather was glorious, too hot for Manhattan, but perfect for long walks on the beach after dark, clear enough to see the stars that I still miss in the city sky. Henry, your knowledge of the constellations surprised me. What exactly did you study in college, and why can't I remember? Why didn't I know you better, living in the room beside yours all year?

I hate to think about the theory you espoused the night we were alone. Was I really so busy with my own life that I didn't look at "the boy next door?" Yes, you were a "Midwestern townie" and I was "upwardly mobile from New York." How awful I felt when you said that. But if I'm going to be honest—and Henry, I'm determined to keep the promise I made you about that—I have to admit there might be a grain or two of truth in your unpleasant assertion.

I hate to think I "underestimated" you, as you suggested so casually on the beach Thursday night. My only defense is that I underestimated myself too. Henry, back in Ann Arbor, you must have thought I was so superficial. Now I feel awful that you saw me that way. I tried to apologize on the beach, but you merely shrugged and threw another log on the fire. Flames lit your face, flickered in your glasses, and threw orange light across your bearded cheeks. Then below your mustache, where your lips were shadowed, your teeth flashed white with a forced smile. That's when I thought I glimpsed the hurt behind your nonchalant attitude.

Henry, I want to apologize for being so dense in college. After these last few weeks with Andrea Thane, I really needed a weekend with you to feel what I've been missing. You know, I was drawn to the Thanes for their intensity—a kind of feverish high—very exciting, like a roller coaster ride. But now I realize there's a driven quality to their energy. Everything feels so different around you, Henry, near your genuine exuberance that seems to well up from someplace deep inside. I can't help thinking there's a weird, sad—maybe even desperate—quality to the Thanes' intensity, as if it's supposed to compensate or distract them from an inner lack. As if something important is missing from the core of their lives. Henry, your energy starts much more quietly than theirs, but it gathers momentum—without drawing attention to itself—and overflows onto the lucky people around you. Thanks for letting me be one of those lucky people.

Part of me wishes I could stay on Fire Island forever instead of going into the office tomorrow, where I'm expecting all hell to break out. The office manager's been gunning for me since Sam went to Tokyo; she'll kill me tomorrow for sure. I'm trying to come up with a viable illness that could force me to rush out of the office without a word. Food poisoning wouldn't last longer than 24 hours. Virus? Stomach flu? I'd better brush up on my acting. Wish me luck.

Lotsa luv and thanks again,

Lara

Lara Leeds | Administrative Assistant
THANE PR INC.
117 Times Square, 3rd Floor, New York, NY 10036
☎direct phone (212) 555-0843
www.ThanePR.com

Subject: home at last
Date: 7/1/2013   4:25 PM
From: *AndreaThane@gmail.com*
To: *SThane@ThanePR.com*

Sam dear,

I'm back in our apartment, and the kitchen looks lovely. Our new granite counters are elegant, while the white-and-yellow backsplash generates a cheerful, hygienic atmosphere. I hope you'll be sharing that sight with me sometime in the near future, my dear.

I heard from Beth—who I think you lately manage to call more frequently than me—that your meeting with Makashi's board of directors went well. (So odd that Monday is already over in Japan.) This morning I stopped by your office with several files I'd unearthed while reorganizing our apartment. They must have been misplaced before construction began and lost in the ensuing upheaval. At any rate, while I was at the office Beth told me you'd scheduled the Makashi contract signing for Wednesday. Wonderful news.

I was hoping you'd come home after that, but I understand from Beth you've planned a stop in Hong Kong. Sam dear, I fear you're acting even more remote than usual—ever since my effusive email. Or was it really the tender night that inspired my missive that abated your normally frequent communications? If I promise to maintain a chilly, critical composure, will you give me a call? I'll be as thorny and uncooperative as a porcupine—word of honor.

Love, Andy

Subject: a personal favor
Date: 7/1/2013   4:35 PM
From: *AndreaThane@gmail.com*
To: *BBlain@ThanePR.com*

Dear Beth,

    Thank you for taking charge of Sam's files for me. It's a pleasure—a luxury really—to have such complete trust in the competence of a friend. Beth, there's no one as organized and thorough as you. Did I mention how much I enjoyed our lunch last week? We mustn't let so long pass before dining together again.

    Beth, I have a favor to ask. And you may well consider it an odd one. But this morning while I was at the office, I couldn't help but overhear you scolding a young woman—Ms. Leeds, I believe. As an act of kindness toward me, could you forgive her this once—whatever her transgressions? Only with the greatest respect and reluctance do I interfere in office matters this way, and I apologize for my intrusion. But this is an issue of some importance to me, and I would be most grateful—and in your debt—if you can help me out.

    Beth, I depend upon your discretion and unflinching loyalty. In a city—and industry—where façade is all and hard work takes second seat to flash, you are one of the few individuals who still behaves in a decent, heartfelt manner. I will always treasure that about you.

Yours, Andrea

Subject: your Manhattan visit
Date: 7/2/2013   9:45 PM
From: *LLeeds@ThanePR.com*
To: *HAltman@AltmanGizmo.com*

Henry,

When I tried your phone, the machine wouldn't take a message. Maybe it's broken? But I'd LOVE you to visit tomorrow. Who cares about short notice? And of course, you're welcome to stay two nights.

Seriously, I'm GLAD you need a place to sleep after the show at the Javitz Center. I'm GRATEFUL to those business associates who insisted you attend at the last minute.

I'll leave my key and your name with the doorman. This way you can arrive any time, unpack, make yourself at home. Listen Henry, I'm sorry to hear Kelly got transferred to London—I mean, if I'm supposed to be? But your email said she'd been hoping to relocate, and you've known that all along. So I shouldn't feel guilty wishing her a speedy bon voyage, safe flight and Godspeed! When's she leaving?

Meantime, the weirdest thing is happening at work. I just don't know what to make of it. Yesterday the office manager seemed like she was going to fire me, put me on probation or <u>something</u>. I mean, she yelled so loudly the whole office heard. (Surprisingly, I didn't die of embarrassment.)

Maybe recent experiences have changed my perspective on maintaining an image. Anyway, today the office manager's quiet as a mouse. She didn't hand down a punishment or even write an official memo. Is it a miracle? Amnesia? Fate intervening on my behalf? Let's hope my reprieve lasts. See you tomorrow.

Lotsa luv,
Lara

Lara Leeds | Administrative Assistant
THANE PR INC.
117 Times Square, 3rd Floor, New York, NY 10036
☎direct phone (212) 555-0843
www.ThanePR.com

H. A.

Noon, 7/3/2013

Hey Lara,

Thanks for leaving your key. It's great being able to drop off my stuff before going to the Javitz Center. (Left my knapsack on the chair in the bedroom.) I like your apartment—not bad for the Upper East Side! And a doorman building, how swanky. Looks like you've arrived, kiddo.

Listen, I'm not sure exactly when I'll be back, but definitely in time for dinner. I'd like to take you out someplace nice, so don't spoil your appetite. What do you think about Italian? My mouth is watering for marinara.

Let's discuss it over a bottle of Pinot Grigio. I hope that's still your favorite because it's cooling in the fridge right now.

Looking forward, see you soon, and all that jazz.

Lotsa luv coming right back at you,

Henry

Subject: sick?
Date: 7/3/2013   12:15 PM
From: *SThane@ThanePR.com*
To: *LLeeds@ThanePR.com*

Lara, I understand you were sick last week. Nothing too serious, I hope? I've been thinking about you—off and on—since last Weds when I heard you ran out of the office. Hmm . . . If I didn't know better, I'd wonder if something nefarious was going on?

Lara, Lara, I'm not a trusting man, but I'm willing to barter. You tell me what's happening, and I promise a free pass. Otherwise, I may have to give Beth license to take whatever actions she considers appropriate. Now keep in mind that you can tell me anything, my sweet. Nothing can shock me. Nothing will offend me. **Nothing**. Lara, this is a **one-time-only, no-holds-barred, no-strings-attached** offer.

Be smart and tell me what's happening. Something started right after I left for Japan. I'm sure of it; I've got a nose for these things. And I noticed you were different the weekend I flew back to NYC—preoccupied even while we were alone, not your usual self. It's hard for a man to keep a handle on things when he's away from home so long. So help me out, and tell the truth. You won't regret it.

Sam
Samuel H. Thane | President
THANE PR INC.
117 Times Square, 3rd Floor, New York, NY 10036
☎direct phone (212) 555-0842
www.ThanePR.com

Subject: the truth
Date: 7/3/2013   2:25 PM
From: *LLeeds@ThanePR.com*
To: *SThane@ThanePR.com*

Hi Sam, I'd actually been wondering why you weren't scolding me. (Not that Beth didn't yell enough for both of you.) Listen, I was really sick last week, but I apologize for bailing on the office. That was unprofessional, and it won't happen again. If you give me another chance, I'll make sure you're not sorry. Sam, I appreciate my job at Thane PR, and I'm sorry if I've done anything to jeopardize it. But perhaps you'll find it in your heart to admit that we both bear some responsibility for that?

Anyway, despite everything—or maybe because of everything—I really must remark on your intimidation strategy. Threatening to give Beth "license" for whatever she thought appropriate? You're the boss, Sam. If you want to fire me, I guess I'll be gone. But, for what it's worth, I find I'm at peace about our relationship. We had fun—a regular roller coaster ride of thrilling highs and lows that I wouldn't change for the world.

So that's the report from New York. There's nothing more to tell. I understand you'll be in Asia till next week, but the whole office knows from Beth that the Makashi contract was finally signed earlier today. So congratulations on all your hard work.

Respectfully, Lara

Lara Leeds | Administrative Assistant
THANE PR INC.
117 Times Square, 3rd Floor, New York, NY 10036
☎direct phone (212) 555-0843
www.ThanePR.com

H. A.

6PM, 7/4/2013

To the Lovely Lady of the House,

Lara, I just ran out to pick up a few things at the supermarket. I'm determined to make us dinner. The restaurant was fun last night, but it's time for an evening alone at home with you. Besides, I have to show off my talents. Bet you didn't know I'm a damn good chef.

By the way, thanks for trying to be quiet this morning. My God, you get up early to work out. But your sofa was really comfortable, and I slept through the whole thing while you crashed around the living room. But what happened after that? You forget something, right?

Because I thought I heard the door slam twice. What kind of hostess are you?

Don't sweat it, kiddo. I'm just giving you a hard time. For fun. That way you won't miss the Thanes too much. Not that I have their expertise at teasing, but perhaps with a little practice . . .

By the way, I bumped into your superintendent and asked him about apartments in this building. Remind me to tell you what he said.a

See you in a few—
Henry

Journal—July 5, 2013

Steak au poivre, wild rice, broccoli gratin—who knew Henry Altman could cook? Last night we shared his gourmet dinner, accompanied by imported beer. Henry was still dressed for the Javitz Center in a white button-down shirt and jeans that hugged his butt. His sandy beard was neatly trimmed, and his brown eyes—fringed by lashes too long and thick to be wasted on a man—were clearly visible with contact lenses. I wore a hot-pink tank-top and a short skirt that showed off my legs. When dinner was over and the dishes cleared, Henry and I settled on the living room sofa, pushing aside the folded blanket and pillow he'd used the night before.

"Do you still indulge?" he asked, removing a joint from his shirt pocket. "I wasn't sure. . . ." He waved the marijuana cigarette between us. "Now that you're so corporate and all."

A sweep of his arm indicated my living room entertainment center, a floor-to-ceiling wall unit that accommodated the TV, surround sound, DVD and CD player I'd purchased from my roommate for a song right before she got married. Henry's shirtsleeves were rolled up to his elbows, his tanned forearms exposed. His fine springy arm hairs were bleached light by the sun, and his white cotton collar opened at the throat into a V of golden tan skin.

"I haven't gotten high in ages." My eyes scanned the shelves I'd filled with books and knickknacks, looking for an ashtray. I found a small glass box; the top of that would do. As I rose to retrieve it, Henry slipped his silver-ringed hand into his pants pocket and pulled out a pack of matches. He lit the joint, and the strong, sweet odor of marijuana stung my nose.

"You forgot to ask," Henry said as I returned with the makeshift ashtray. "But your superintendent showed me a

studio apartment today; it was depressingly small."
Between his sandy blond beard and mustache—both
lightened by the sun—his lips looked red as clay. His
ringed hand held the joint to his mouth; I watched him suck
the smoke in. "There aren't any more one bedroom
apartments available," he concluded, passing the joint to
me.

"Rats." I took a hit and started coughing. "Damn," I
sputtered, doubling over. "It's been such a long time."

"It has," Henry agreed with a yearning note that
made me wonder if he was referring to the weed.

"Would you really consider living in this building?" I
asked, as my coughing subsided.

"Sure." He shrugged, taking the joint from my hand.
A lock of blond hair fell over his tanned forehead, and he
eyed me above a plume of smoke.

As I met his frank gaze, something tweaked my
chest, and for a moment, I felt older than Henry, although
we're both 24.

"You've made quite a life for yourself," he said then,
bringing the joint to his lips.

"I have?"

"Look around." Waving a tanned arm, he indicated
the high tech living room furniture my roommate had left
behind: the beige canvas sofa, glass and chrome coffee
table, standing halogen lamps, and ecru area rug. "A one
bedroom apartment on the Upper East Side." He inhaled
the pot with a hiss. "Three years after college, Lara, and
you're already advancing up the corporate ladder, living in
a doorman building." Expertly, he held the smoke in his
lungs while passing the joint to me.

"Yeah," I said, taking a hit. "_If_ I can actually afford
this place by myself. _If_ I don't get fired over my recent
escapades."

"You're a cat," Henry said. "You'll land on your feet."
He took the joint back from my hand and inhaled deeply,
closing his eyes.

Henry's eyelids seemed rimmed with black where
his dark lashes met the pale lids in a line. His sandy blond
head leaned back against the sofa. In my apartment, his
bearded face looked both familiar and strange. Of course,
I'd kissed those clay-red lips three years before, and my
mouth had felt the tickle of his straw-colored mustache. I'd
tasted his skin and smelled his hair, both herbal scented
from the health food store products he'd used.

"Meow," I said on impulse, leaning close enough to
make the noise near his ear. "Rrrr," I rumbled an imitation
purr.

"Ruff, ruff." H.'s brown eyes opened; his tongue
lolled out, and he took a few panting breaths.

"Meow?" I posed it like a question, tilting my head.

"Ruff, ruff!" he gave me a lopsided grin along with
the end of our smoldering joint.

I took a last long hit before abandoning the stub end
to the ashtray. Then, still holding the smoke deep in my
lungs, I pulled my legs up onto the couch and arranged
myself on all fours. On my hands and knees, I nuzzled my
cheek into H.'s white cotton shoulder, the way cats
sometimes graze their furry faces over people's calves. The
pleasant prickle of a marijuana high was settling over my
shoulders as I let out what I hoped was a melodic mew.

"Urrr," came Henry's answering doggy growl, low
and throaty, an invitation.

"Ra!" was quick and coy from me, an exclamation of
delight. My nose nudged his neck; my lips brushed his skin.

Half-growl, half-giggle, Henry's response made me
laugh.

I watched the spotlights from my ceiling track glisten
and bounce off his sandy hair and noticed it wasn't sand-
colored at all, but myriad shades from wheat to butter, from

lemon yellow to the palest brown. As I looked closely at Henry's hair, the air between us thickened. The many hued strands fell over his tanned forehead, curled around his ears and the collar of his white cotton shirt.

"Why are you looking at me like that?" he asked.

"No reason." I sat back on my haunches, giggling like a child.

"Lara, come over here," he said in a fake stern tone. "I need to have a talk with you." Grinning, he beckoned with a crooked finger.

"Mmm," I said, giggling "I don't think so." Reaching for his neck above the V of golden tan skin, I asked, "Are you ticklish?"

"Try me." He threw back his blond head to bare his throat, and my fingers came in for the kill.

I feathered the hollow of his throat, the sides and back of his neck. "How do you keep such a poker face?" I asked when his expression didn't change.

"Zen concentration," his tone was deadpan, but beneath his mustache, his lips began to twitch.

"We'll see about that." My fingers danced over his belly, covered by his white cotton shirt. "Unless I've lost my touch."

"I doubt that." Henry let out a low chuckle. "I doubt that very much."

"Zen's overrated." I stopped tickling and sat back on my heels. "But we could try some Tantra if you like. I've got a book about it somewhere."

"I'll bet you do." He shot me a glance I couldn't decipher. "Know what we need?" he asked next, standing up. "Music. Let's take this surround sound system of yours for a test drive."

I followed Henry to the entertainment center. "With your set up, it's a sin not to listen to jazz. What about some Coltrane?"

"Okay," I said, shuffling through his iPod playlist. "I don't really know him."

"Well then, you're in for a treat."

Henry retrieved his iPod from his knapsack and hooked it up to my sound system. "*My Favorite Things*," he announced with a grin as the opening saxophone notes issued from my speakers.

Moments later I recognized a melody from my childhood. "Wait a minute," I said. "Isn't this Mary Poppins? No, I mean Julie Andrews. That movie where the nun becomes a nanny?"

Henry laughed. "We're way out of Julie Andrews' territory now." We were still standing in front of the wall unit, and he gestured expansively over the living room, indicating the startling twists and turns of music that had literally begun to surround us.

"I always think—when I hear this piece—that we're listening to Coltrane's favorite things right now," H. said. "You know, the way he plays with the music, riffing off the melody, taking it to the edge. Listen to how he experiments, pushing off from that original tune, going on a musical tangent so to speak, and then circling back in on himself, returning to the familiar theme. See?" His brown eyes were clear and intelligent, peering into mine. "At the chorus, Coltrane gives the old melody a run through, and then he goes riffing off again."

"I didn't know you were into jazz," I said, smiling at Henry's enthusiasm and wondering what else I didn't know about him.

"Yeah." He shrugged. "Listen to this part. See how Coltrane stretches My Favorite Things to its limit, teasing and honoring the melody at the same time. He loves to remix and rearrange, adding texture and range that the original composer never dreamed of."

"Wow," I said as the saxophone blared a high note that almost sounded like a screech. "I've heard the sax

118

compared to a human voice," I said, thinking the screech felt like a cry of longing, feeling the music with the surface of my skin and the edges of my teeth.

"Hear that shrieky part?" Henry asked. "That's Coltrane trying to play higher than the highest register." He took my hand and led me back to the sofa. "You see, the sax has three registers, but Coltrane likes to push the envelope, playing both higher and lower than the instrument was intended to go."

"Much more exciting than 'raindrops on roses and whiskers on kittens,'" I commented with a laugh as we settled on the canvas couch. I stretched out my bare legs, resting my bare feet with crossed ankles on the coffee table, tugging my short skirt an inch or two down my thighs.

"Much more exciting." Henry's ringed hand patted my knee.

"I'm all in favor of stretching limits," I said, exaggeratedly flipping my long dark hair and batting my eyelashes at Henry.

"Yes." His hand reached under my leg, into the hidden crease behind my knee, ran over the curve of my calf and back again. "For example, I could keep moving up." His fingers slid toward my inner thigh and crept as high as the hem of my skirt. "Or this could be considered a limit." His hand stopped.

"We could play on the edge," I suggested with a giggle.

"Now, how would that look?" Henry's hand moved a little higher, under the hem of my loose skirt. "I mean, sometimes it's hard to know where the edge is."

"Mmm." I uncrossed my ankles. "That is a problem." My thighs spread, making more room for his hand to slip between them.

"And then the edge can change," Henry continued, sliding his hand between my thighs, moving it further up. "The edge is flexible, elastic."

"Yes." I gave a little pelvic thrust, thinking about the elastic that held my panties up. "And the great thing about elastic is that it gives."

"So it does." He tilted his blond head, ran his brown eyes over my face until they came to rest on my mouth.

I licked my upper lip with a slow tongue and found my mouth had gone dry—probably from the pot. Henry's face moved toward mine, but I couldn't kiss him with a papery tongue.

"Water," I said, after giving him a peck on the lips. "I need to get some water."

"I'll go," he offered, but I'd already risen from his lap.

Then somehow I miscalculated the distance to the coffee table and dashed my shin against the edge of the glass top. Falling back, I let out a howl. Henry's hands rose fast to catch me, and an instant later I lay across his lap, sideways in his arms like a baby.

"There, there," he murmured, while I rubbed my shin.

"Holy cow," I exclaimed, starting to giggle. "That really hurt."

Henry rocked me a little; I felt small in his arms. "Poor baby," he said.

The side of my face nestled his chest. Beneath the white cotton shirt, his pectoral muscles felt firm on my cheek. I reached for his bicep under his shirtsleeve and squeezed. "Wow," I admired. "You've gotten strong."

"Yeah." His tone went sheepish, but I could tell he was proud. "Weight training, it's a good balance with my running."

Sitting on Henry's lap, my butt sensed his thighs, muscular from running. Leaning into his chest, my side felt his firm abdomen; my arm slipped around his neck where the lightly tanned skin looked—it suddenly hit me—especially taut and youthful.

"Let me carry you to the kitchen," he said then, rising from the sofa with me in his arms.

Carrying me seemed effortless for Henry, and in the kitchen, he opened the refrigerator, still holding me in his arms. There were two bottles of Poland Springs water on the fridge door; I took them out. H. brought me back into the living room and gently lowered me to the sofa.

Then, opening my water bottle and handing it to me, he began in a serious tone, "Lara, there's something I wanted to tell you. Something I think you should know." I took a long swallow before setting my water down on the coffee table.

"What's up?" I tented my knees and wrapped my arms around them.

Above his blond beard, Henry's cheeks flushed; his brown eyes worked to stay steady on mine. "It's something I should have told you three years ago, back in Ann Arbor."

"Really?" My arms loosened around my knees. "What?"

Piano keys sounded; music swelled; Henry's voice came out low beneath it. "The way I always felt about you."

A silver shiver shot through my giggly marijuana haze. "But you were in love with Terry." My voice seemed to pierce the music.

"I know you thought that." Our eyes locked.

I unclasped my knees and reached out, moving close enough to stroke Henry's many-hued hair and beard.

"I should have told you." For a moment, his head lowered; he spoke into his lap. "Not that it would have changed anything." His brown eyes raised; wide and round, they confronted mine.

"No," I admitted, still stroking his hair. "It wouldn't have changed anything."

"But now . . . ?" His question hung in the air; like Coltrane's favorite riffs, it twirled and spiraled around us.

I leaned forward to kiss his mouth. Henry's lips met mine, and his tongue came out to play.

While kissing, we moved closer on the sofa, until our bodies pressed together and our arms encircled each other's backs. Henry's chest was firm and warm against my breasts; his back felt lean and muscular. He still smelled herbal, male, and unaccountably young. Is young a smell? It seemed to be last night. Young seemed a smell, and— although I hadn't thought of the Thanes as old when I was with them—I'd missed it. Without being aware, I'd missed the tender fumbling and tentative gestures that sometimes opened the door to sex.

Last night Henry and I kissed on the sofa for a long time. But when he finally reached under my tank-top and faltered with the clasp of my bra, I laughed with joy. Then I decided to tantalize him. Sliding off the sofa, swaying my hips in time to the music in their short flouncy skirt, I stood in front of Henry on the ecru area rug, letting the soles of my bare feet revel in its velvety knap. On impulse, I spun a circle until my short skirt rose up like a ballerina's tutu. Henry clapped; the speaker system throbbed with piano, sax, percussion, and bass, making me want to move. A spaghetti strap from my hot-pink tank-top fell off my shoulder as my hips ground in a circle. That's when I thought of doing a striptease.

There wasn't much to remove, but I stretched it out, slithering out of my tank-top, twirling it over my head. Henry gave a cat call, and I blew him a kiss. The saxophone groaned as I loosened the button at the waist of my skirt, and when that bright fluff of pink fell to the floor, the instrument let out a wail. Cavorting across the living room in my petal pink bra and panties, my two-for-one lingerie seemed more than adequate. On tiptoe, I played the half-naked ballerina until I spied an old penny on my knickknack shelf. Then I switched to belly dancing, sticking the penny in my navel and trying to keep it there while I swiveled my hips. But that coin trick is harder than it looks, and the penny kept falling out, giving Henry and me the giggles.

Maybe it was the pot, maybe it was Henry, but for some reason, I felt blissfully un-self conscious. When the music reached its next crescendo, I unsnapped my bra, peeled it off, and ended with an exuberant toss. Then I fashioned a g-string by folding the back of my scant panties into a narrow thong.

On the sofa before me, Henry was grinning like the cat that ate the bird. Hips gyrating, I approached and retreated, offered teasing pelvic thrusts until Henry reached into his jean pocket and pulled out a twenty dollar bill. He folded it and stashed it in my panties the next time I came close enough. That made me think of lap dancing, and I decided to wriggle over the sofa, teasing him with my breasts. I brought alternate nipples close to Henry's mouth, grazing his lips for just an instant before pulling away. The sensitivity of my nipples surprised me. They weren't tender or sore, yet the lightest touch of Henry's lips felt exquisite. The merest brush of contact seemed electrical, and my nipples sparked, reaching, begging for his mouth even as, laughing, I spun away.

When at last I decided I'd tortured us both enough, I settled nearly naked on my knees before Henry and began unbuttoning his shirt. First his golden tan chest was revealed with its sparse, but springy sun-bleached hair. Then my hands moved down to his belt buckle. My fingers worked it open and unzipped his fly. "Stand up, please," I whispered.

Henry rose, and I pulled his jeans down to his ankles. Without a word, he stepped out.

"I want to look at you," I said then, moving back a few inches.

There stood Henry Altman in his navy jockey shorts, his muscled arms hanging lose at his sides, his silver-ringed hands empty. His brown eyes were wide; his terra cotta lips parted. Here I am, his face seemed to say.

"Yes," I replied. "There you are." And an up-rush of tenderness welled in my chest, surged beneath my breast bone, up to the hollow of my throat.

I walked the few steps to where he stood and knelt before him again. Reaching up, I pulled his underwear down; Henry's erection sprung out. I licked my lips and kissed the swollen head. Then, grasping the bottom of the shaft with a firm hand, I encircled the top with my mouth. Tenderness flooded my chest as I enveloped and tongued him.

Henry's hand found my head; his touch was light as a blessing. Maybe it was the pot, but I visualized his shape as my mouth tasted it. I saw the ridges and smooth parts, the exact form of the top—like a mushroom—and the length with its vertical veins. My lips slid over the easy, eager-to-bursting hardness of a young man's erection. And as I licked and sucked, my tongue read Henry the way fingertips read Braille. Finally, when I knew he was getting ready to explode, I stopped, rose, and led him to the bedroom by his silver ringed hand.

There I lay down on the bed; sprawling my arms and legs, looking up at his big brown eyes, I said, "Do with me what you will."

Subject: apartment sharing
Date: 7/06/2013   11:25 PM
From: *LLeeds@ThanePR.com*
To: *HAltman@AltmanGizmo.com*

Henry,

What a sweet email! And you were the perfect guest. Don't
ya know? I miss you already. Wish I could've convinced
you to stay longer, but I understand you've got to look after
your beach house, especially on a big holiday weekend.

Henry, I need to ask you something—seriously—now that
we're not stoned. Would you really consider sharing this
apartment, the way we lucid-dreamed it in bed late
Thursday night? Bunking with me on Second Avenue, in a
doorman building—are you sure you can take it? Nasty
New York is worlds away from little academic Ann Arbor.
Do you think you can bear—presuming my current
employment survives my boss's return—watching me climb
"the corporate ladder?" Will you have feelings if I keep on
working for Sam?

What if we hate each other after a month or two? What if it
all turns into a mess? I'm not actually being rhetorical here.
I really want to know. Tell me your feelings on these issues.
Take time to think if you want. For once, I'm not in rush.

Our night together was special.

Love, Lara

Lara Leeds | Administrative Assistant
THANE PR INC.
117 Times Square, 3rd Floor, New York, NY 10036
☎direct phone (212) 555-0843
www.ThanePR.com

Subject: difficult
Date: 7/08/2013   10:25 AM
From: *AndreaThane@gmail.com*
To: *SThane@ThanePR.com*

Sam dear,

   This is going to be a difficult email. I've been debating since yesterday whether to write with my news or wait three days and impart it in person. Finally I decided to afford you the same privileges I enjoyed: privacy and the right to your own unbridled reaction—whatever that may be. You deserve the time to think, my dear, or *feel*, before you deal with me. And, to be perfectly honest, I prefer not to watch your handsome face react to my report. So you're duly warned, my love. I need not tell you to sit down.

   Darling, it is sometimes said that no good deed goes unpunished. Perhaps the same assertion should be made about good times, however precious and infrequent. It seems our evening of carnal delight and a broken condom has—against all odds—resulted in pregnancy. Yes Sam, I'm certain. (I can hear that question across thousands of miles.) Even before the home pregnancy test, I knew. (Don't forget, I've been pregnant before; it's quite an unforgettable sensation.) Sam dear, you needn't reply right away. Let the news sink in, and call me when you're ready.

Love, Andy

Subject: custom order
Date: 7/08/2013   11:03 AM
From: *SThane@ThanePR.com*
To: *DKlien@LexingtonFlowers.com*

Sam Thane here. I'm out of town and need one of your custom arrangements. 4 dozen long-stemmed, red roses delivered today **ASAP** to my home address along with 1 gallon of dill pickles and 1 gallon of **Häagen-Dazs** chocolate ice cream. Sorry to send you to the supermarket, but I depend on you to handle this custom order with the same expertise you've demonstrated in the past.

Important: please do not make separate deliveries. I need these items to arrive together in a tasteful array.

Charge the corporate account. Any problems, verify with Beth Blain. And please include the following note:

Darling Andy,

I'm on the first plane out of Hong Kong. See you in less than 24 hours.

Forever, Sam

Samuel H. Thane | President
THANE PR INC.
117 Times Square, 3rd Floor, New York, NY 10036
☎direct phone (212) 555-0842
www.ThanePR.com

Subject: your continued employment
Date: 7/08/2013   11:15 AM
From: *SThane@ThanePR.com*
To: *LLeeds@ThanePR.com*

Lara,

I just spoke to Beth on the phone, and unaccountably, she's become your greatest supporter. As a result you will get another chance. I advise you to be careful with it. Re: you're being "at peace" with our past, I'm happy to hear it, and I rely on your maturity and discretion. I fly home today and will see you—along with all other Thane PR employees— Friday at the office.

Whatever has been disturbing your work these last few weeks is now concluded, I trust. Going forward, I expect your behavior to be exemplary. I will be extending a warm thank you to all employees who participated in the Makashi project at the office party. This will be your opportunity to demonstrate a change in attitude and renewed dedication to your work.

Lara, upon my return, I fully anticipate encountering once again the competent and professional approach you initially applied to your tasks at Thane PR.

Sam Thane

Samuel H. Thane | President
THANE PR INC.
117 Times Square, 3rd Floor, New York, NY 10036
☎direct phone (212) 555-0842
www.ThanePR.com

Subject: Miracles and Madness
Date: 7/11/2013 3:15 PM
From: *LLeeds@ThanePR.com*
To: *HAltman@AltmanGizmo.com*

Henry,

I tried your phone, but got the darn machine. Where are
you? Listen, I know I'm going to see you tonight, but I have
news that just won't wait. Firstly, I figured out how to
rearrange the living room to free up that corner you're
going to need for a work station. Yes, Yours Truly
dismantled the leftmost shelves of the wall unit ALL BY
HERSELF and stacked them on the opposite side of the
room where we thought they'd look best. Next time you're
in town, we'll hang some brackets to support them or
whatever. But I've cleared a great space for your tools
etc.—I know you're going to like it.

Maybe you'll come back with me Sunday night and stay in
the city midweek? But don't worry, I won't blame you if you
choose Fire Island over my marvelous company; the
Manhattan heat is insufferable. So long as I know you're
moving in for real after Labor Day, I'm happy as a clam.

Number two: Right now the office party is going full tilt
boogie; I just skipped out to contact you. Of course, you
know Sam's back from Asia, but here's the part that will
blow your mind: ANDY'S HERE AND SHE'S ALL OVER
HIM. Yes, the Nordic Ice Queen is all lovey-dovey with her
husband! Henry, if I live to be a thousand, I'll never
understand those two. Honestly, you have to see it to
believe it, but Andy and Sam are standing at the center of
the party, arms around each other's shoulders, shooting
one another sly glances as if they've just fallen in love. And

Beth hovers around them like a frumpy, middle-aged, guardian angel. It's a riot to watch.

I wish you were here to see it with me. The fabulous Andrea Thane—impeccably dressed as always in a cream-colored linen sheath that molds to her body and a tailored jacket to match—is laughing and chatting with admiring personnel. As if this behavior were perfectly natural, as if she often showed up at company events to create good will and hobnob with the staff. And beside her, the profligate Sam Thane seems her greatest admirer of all. (Unless you want to count Beth, who actually appears besotted with both Thanes. Is it possible to be in love with a couple? Or perhaps that's a question I shouldn't ask?)

Thankfully, the Thanes are acting cordial but aloof with me. Although Sam's eyes do move in a speculative way from Andy's face to mine every now and then. But the neutral expression I'm maintaining should make my mentor proud, if she notices it. But Andy's moon round face is so poised I can't tell whether or not she's monitoring those interchanges. Oh Henry, Henry, *mon ami*, it's a miracle I survived this June without losing my mind or my job. I'll cut out of here as soon as possible and head straight for the Fire Island ferry. Hopefully, I'll make the 6:15. But I want you to know that—with all my misadventures and machinations—you are the most exciting thing that's happening to me now.

Love, Lara

Lara Leeds | Administrative Assistant
THANE PR INC.
117 Times Square, 3rd Floor, New York, NY 10036
☎direct phone (212) 555-0843
www.ThanePR.com

ACKNOWLEDGMENTS

I'd like to thank writing coach Jacob Miller for helping me birth the first draft of this novella. My gratitude also goes to David Rhodes for his help with book design and to Doreen Meyers for her assistance in every aspect of production. In addition, I'd like to thank Gary Lesser for urging me forward, as well as Marguerite Elisofon, Lynne Feldman, and my brother Michael Cohen for their endless loving support.

CPSIA information can be obtained
at www.ICGtesting.com
Printed in the USA
FFOW05n0250070514